Magnificent

By Lucy Felthouse

Text Copyright 2021 © Lucy Felthouse.

All Rights Reserved.

With the exception of quotes used in reviews, this book may not be reproduced or used in whole or in part by any means existing without written permission from the aforementioned author.

Warning: The unauthorised reproduction or distribution of this copyrighted work is illegal. No part of this book may be scanned, uploaded or distributed via the Internet or any other means, electronic or print, without the author's written permission.

This book is a work of fiction and any resemblance to persons, living or dead is purely coincidental. The characters are productions of the author's imagination and used fictitiously.

Ditched

"This can't be fucking right!" said Lance Corporal Michael Scott, checking his map for the umpteenth time.

"I can assure you, Scott, that it fucking is," responded his colleague, Private Damien Stone. He nudged the other man, pointed to a place on his own map, then raised his arm and indicated a rise in the ground in the near distance. "See, that's *that* long barrow, so we are in the right place."

Looking at the barrow—one of the many on Salisbury Plain—then down at the map, and finally at his compass, Scott had to agree. "So where the fuck are they, then?"

Stone had no answer for that one. He looked up into the lightening sky, which in the distance was tinged with pink, but saw no sign of their pick-up helicopter. Straining to hear even the faintest sound of rotor blades, Stone remained silent. Hearing nothing, he shrugged. "Dunno. Perhaps we got the time wrong?"

"I hope not, otherwise they've gone without us!"

"Nah. We're early, if anything. The sun's only just coming up."

Sighing, Scott stuffed his map and compass into a pocket and said, "Well, I guess we'd better find somewhere to shelter. I don't like the look of *that*."

The *that* he was talking about was an ominous-looking black cloud being buffeted in their direction by the wind, which was picking up rapidly.

"With you on that one."

On an unspoken command, they immediately split up and

started to look around for somewhere they could keep out of the wind and imminent rain. It wasn't long before Scott shouted out, and Stone immediately turned and headed in the direction of his colleague's voice.

When Stone arrived, Scott had already removed his backpack and dropped it into the ditch he'd found and was striding down the slope to join it. Luckily, there'd been no rain over the past few days so the ground was dry. If the coming rainstorm ended up being heavy, it was entirely possible they'd get wet arses, and much more besides, but for now at least they'd be reasonably comfortable.

Following his colleague's example, Stone shrugged off his pack. Scott was standing with his arms out, ready to catch it. Stone tossed it, then gave a curt nod of thanks before heading into the ditch.

Once there, he spotted scrub covering a couple of sizeable rocks, meaning they would at least be able to sit down. It would have to rain pretty damn hard for the water level in the ditch to get as high as the top of the rocks, so they'd be all right until the chopper arrived.

He hoped.

Stone pulled out his switchblade and began hacking at the scrub to clear it away. The roots and branches were thick in places. He soon became impatient, grabbed a handful and yanked—an action he quickly regretted.

"Fuck me!" he yelled, dropping the blade and cradling his injured hand with the other one. A deep, nasty scratch, flanked by a couple of more superficial ones, striped his palm. Blood welled up.

"All right, Stone?" Scott had been so busy scanning the sky for a sign of their transport that he hadn't seen what had happened.

"Do I fucking look all right?" Stone snapped, moving towards his backpack to get a bandage and something to clean the wound.

"Chill out, mate. It's not exactly a landmine, is it?"

Scott's attempt at humour—tasteless as it was—only served to inflame Stone's temper further. He shot Scott a glare that would have turned a lesser man to stone, yet said nothing, then opened his bag to unearth the medical supplies, trying not to smear blood everywhere. It wasn't easy.

Sighing, Scott nudged Stone out of the way. "Come on, mate. Let me get it for you."

Muttering, Stone allowed his colleague to retrieve the kit. His hand was still bleeding, though not as freely. A glance up at the sky told him they were still completely alone on the plain. Where the hell was the fucking helicopter?

Before he got chance to wonder too much about it, Scott stepped in front of him, medical kit in hand. Taking the wrist of Stone's injured hand, Scott looked at the cut. He then tore open and used a medicated wipe to clean it, biting back a smirk when Stone hissed as the chemicals went into the wound and stung him.

Finishing the job with a neatly-fastened bandage and a clap on the shoulder, Scott said, "Okay, mate. You're all set."

"Thanks," Stone replied, flexing his hand to make sure the bandage wasn't too tight or too loose. "Shoulda' been more bloody careful, shouldn't I?"

Grinning good-naturedly, Scott spread his arms in a placating manner. "Hey, I didn't say a word."

"Just as well. I'm not in the mood."

"I noticed."

The words brought a wry grin to Stone's face. "Oh, fuck off. You know what I'm like."

"Too right I do. You're a miserable bastard. That's the first time I've seen you smile in ages."

"Charming."

"Just telling it like it is."

His grin fading, Stone asked, "Am I really that bad? Tell me honestly."

Scott raised his eyebrows. "You want *brutal* honesty?"

Stone nodded.

"In that case, yes. Don't get me wrong, you're damn good at your job, but you come across as a grumpy fucker who resents having to take orders. Especially from me."

Stone tilted his head to one side, considering what his colleague—and superior—had just said. Then he nodded slowly as he came to the realisation Scott was right. "You know, that's a pretty fair assessment. I *don't* like taking orders—and for some reason, you always rub me up the wrong way. Most of the time, I want to tell you to go fuck yourself."

"Don't you think you might be in the wrong job then, mate? The line of work we're in, we all have to take orders."

"No, I'm not in the wrong job. I fucking love what I do, it's just I'd rather go with my own instincts and intelligence than have to do what straitlaced teacher's pets like you tell me."

"Hey," Scott said, clenching his fists, "I may be a straitlaced teacher's pet, but I'm still your fucking superior. And I always will be, if you don't change your attitude. You might think you're some kind of rebel, but this isn't playing army in the garden with your friends any more. This is real, and not taking orders can be the difference between life and death. And not just your life, either. Other people's. So just you remember that."

Stone held his hands up in supplication, wincing as the sudden movement made his wound ache. "Sorry, Scott. I know you're right. And I'm doing my best to suck it up and be a good soldier, all right? So help me out, yeah, and give me a nudge if I'm stepping out of line."

Scott relaxed his position, then turned his back on Stone and walked along the ditch a little way.

Stone grimaced. He'd known this exercise was going to be a nightmare. Not just because it was a drop off in the middle of nowhere with the task being to find a rendezvous point and be picked up—not exactly challenging, in Stone's opinion—but because they'd teamed him up with Scott. Of all the people the powers that be could have chosen, they had to choose *him*. He was a damn good soldier, which was how he'd achieved the rank of Lance Corporal so quickly, but Stone's problem with him had nothing to do with his rank or achievements.

It had to do with the fact he was massively attracted to him, and had been ever since he'd met him. Stone had kept his bisexuality quiet when he joined the forces—there were still enough prejudiced people out there that could make his life a misery—but the more time he spent in Scott's company, the more difficult it became. He was just grateful they'd been dropped off only a few hours ago, making it necessary to keep moving until they found the pick-up point. If they'd been required to do an overnighter, he really didn't know how he'd have coped with having to try to sleep with Scott mere inches away.

Things were becoming pretty difficult right now, in fact. The past few hours they'd been on the move continually, so Stone's mind had mostly been on the exercise—with the occasional thoughts about how good Scott looked in uniform. But now, he had nothing to distract him, except for keeping an eye and ear out for the helicopter. As a result, his libido was ramping up. He hadn't had sex—with a woman or a man—for God knows how long, and watching Scott pace up and down the ditch, deep in thought, was making him painfully aware of the fact. Not to mention painfully hard.

He hadn't realised just how intently he'd been staring at Scott until the other man turned around and caught him doing it.

"What the fuck, man?" Scott said, walking towards him. "Were you staring at me?"

The look on Scott's face told Stone it was pointless denying it. Instead, he shrugged, hoping he'd let it go.

No such luck.

"I asked you a question. Or am I to take your silence as a yes?"

Stone was in the shit, no matter what he said. He pulled himself up to his full height—which was still a few inches shorter than Scott—and looked him square in the eyes. "So what if I was?"

Scott frowned. "Are you trying to tell me you bat for the other team, mate?"

"No," Stone replied, matter of factly, "I bat for both teams."

The other man's eyebrows almost disappeared into his hairline. Several seconds passed and the two men stared at each other. Stone was on edge, not sure what Scott's reaction was going to be to his confession, but just wishing he'd get it over with. He was either going to get laughed at or punched. Either way it backed up his reasons for keeping his sexuality a secret. He clenched his fists, then arched an eyebrow, inviting a response.

Scott shook his head as though ridding himself of a thought, then his expression of surprise disappeared. Only to be replaced by one Stone would never have expected, not in a million years. A predatory grin twisted Scott's lips, and he moved closer to the shorter man. "Well," Scott said, his grin widening, "that's *very* interesting."

"It is?" Stone frowned, still half-expecting a punch in the face. Scott had never shown any inclination towards homophobia before, but then Stone had never told him he liked men before.

"Yes," Scott moved closer still, until they were almost toe to toe, "because I happen to bat for both sides, too."

Stone's jaw dropped. He couldn't believe it—Scott liked men, too? The blond, blue eyed, muscular, towering hottie was bi? And even more strangely, it appeared Scott was interested in *him*, too. Either that or he'd suddenly forgotten about the unspoken personal space rules between people who weren't intimate.

"Y-you do?"

Instead of replying, Scott slipped his hand behind Stone's head and pulled him in for a kiss. Stone's semi immediately snapped to attention and, after spending a couple of seconds wondering if he'd somehow fallen asleep and was dreaming, he returned the other man's kiss. A thought popped into his head that they might be caught—and the consequences would be so severe they didn't even bear thinking about—but then he shoved it away, reasoning with himself that they were the only people for miles, and if the helicopter approached, they'd hear it before they could see it. Therefore the people in the chopper wouldn't be able to see them, either. And by the time they could, the two men would be standing metres apart, acting normally. Probably.

Having put his mind at rest, Stone relaxed and allowed himself to fully enjoy the kiss. And what a kiss it was. A combination of having fancied Scott for ages; thinking it would never happen because the other man was straight; and the fact they were effectively making out in work time made an already super-hot kiss positively molten. His cock pressed insistently against the inside of his boxers and combats, a firm reminder that he hadn't used it in a while.

And, as Scott pulled away then dropped to his knees, Stone concluded there was a very real possibility his dry spell was over.

A spot of rain on his face made him look up. The ominous cloud was now directly over them and he was sure that any minute now it was going to make its presence well and truly known. But, given he was just about to receive a blowjob from the hottest guy in the garrison, he decided it could piss it down for all he cared. At this moment in time, getting his cock into the blond's mouth was far more important.

Scott pulled eagerly at Stone's combats and boxers, releasing his cock from its material prison. It pointed enthusiastically upward, rock hard and with a bead of precum at its reddened tip. The sudden exposure of his private parts to the chilly air made Stone shudder. Then he grunted as the chill was chased away by the hot mouth engulfing his shaft. He reached down and gripped Scott's head—careful not to put any pressure on his cut—guiding the other man's mouth further onto his cock and resisting the temptation to thrust. He didn't know if Scott could deep-throat, but hopefully he'd find out soon enough.

A particularly powerful gust of wind rushed across the plain and buffeted around the parts of Stone's body which weren't protected by the ditch. He swayed a little, and Scott reached up and grabbed his hips to steady him. Stone groaned—the way Scott's large hands gripped him, taking possession of his body, was almost as arousing as the expert way he was sucking his cock. He closed his eyes and threw his head back, tumbling into bliss as the blond bobbed his mouth up and down on his shaft, using his tongue to stimulate it.

Scott pulled back, concentrating on sucking and licking at the meaty head of Stone's cock as he circled his hand around the base of his shaft and pumped it.

The wind gusted again, and this time it brought a heavier raincloud with it. Stone's upturned face caught the first of the droplets, and he smiled and opened his mouth, then stuck out his tongue to catch them. It reminded him just how exposed he and Scott were, partaking in sexual acts in the middle of Salisbury Plain. Rather than worrying him, it turned him on all the more.

Rolling his head forward, he tightened his grip on Scott, hardly feeling the twinge in his palm, and canted his hips, encouraging the blond to suck him harder, faster.

Scott made a humming noise as Stone's cock thrust further into his mouth, almost into his throat. The vibrations across Stone's shaft made his eyes roll back in his head. If Scott carried on like this for much longer, he was going to come. Not that coming was a bad thing, of course, but he didn't want his climax to be the end of their encounter, and he had no idea if Scott felt the same. Perhaps he'd regret what they'd done, and refuse to speak of it ever again? Or maybe he'd throw that punch Stone had been expecting all along.

The tingling at the base of his cock and the tightening of his ballsac told him he wouldn't have to wait too much longer to find out.

A few more bobs of Scott's head and Stone was there. His climax hit with astonishing ferocity and he let out a roar as his spunk shot into Scott's mouth. The rain continued to fall, soaking his hair, face and clothes, but he didn't notice. He was oblivious to everything except the climax taking over his body. He thought he was never going to stop coming, but Scott didn't pull away, or gag. He swallowed every last drop and only disengaged when Stone's balls stopped emptying. He rolled back onto his heels and looked up at Stone with a satisfied expression.

"Good?" he asked.

Stone let out a laugh of disbelief. "Are you kidding? What do you fucking think? I can't remember the last time I came so hard. Or so much."

"Glad to be of service." Scott winked and stood up, wincing as his knees cracked with the sudden movement. "Now, how do you fancy returning the favour? Do you bottom?"

After taking in the unmistakeable bulge in Scott's combats, Stone returned his gaze to the blond's face and smirked. "For you, yeah. Now get it out."

An intense look crossed Scott's face, and suddenly his eyes were full of intent. "I'll get it out, you bend over that rock." He nodded his head in the direction of the rocks Stone had been trying to clear when he'd cut his hand.

"Yes, sir." Stone tipped a mock salute and moved over to the rock before letting his combats and boxers fall to his ankles. He waited until Scott was up close behind him before bending over and exposing his arse to the other man's gaze—and cock. It was a damn good job he was still so horny—they had no lube, and he'd never taken anyone without it before.

Scott bent over his back and murmured into his ear, "You know," Stone felt a wet finger probing his arse, "that's the first time in ages you've actually shown me the respect I deserve, according to my rank."

Stone groaned as his hole stretched around the penetration, then ground out, "Well, if you keep making me come like you just did... unh... I'll call you whatever you like."

With a bark of laughter, Scott replied, "I'll hold you to that. Now, are you ready? If I don't get inside your tight little arse soon, I think I might burst."

Unable to speak as the finger pumped slowly in and out of him, Stone nodded frantically. He sucked in a breath as the digit was removed and the blunt end of Scott's prick pressed against his ring. Gritting his teeth, he pushed back against it and gasped as the head of the blond's cock entered him.

Scott grunted, then laughed. "Eager, aren't we? You *do* like cock, don't you?"

"I thought we'd already established that," Stone replied breathlessly. "Now stop talking and fuck me."

"With pleasure."

The rain grew harder, pounding onto their exposed skin, rolling and dripping off, but Stone really didn't care. All he could think about was the thick cock inching into his back passage, and the gorgeous man it belonged to. He could hardly believe this was happening. How on earth had he gone from fancying a bloke he thought was straight to fucking him on Salisbury Plain in the space of a few hours?

"Fuck," Scott said, digging his fingertips into Stone's hips, "you are so tight. At this rate, I'm gonna come in two strokes."

Stone felt the other man's balls brush against his perineum. He was buried inside him to the hilt, and boy, didn't he know it. His anus was stretched wide, and he was hard again. "Hold on for me, won't you? If you hit the right spot enough times, I may be joining you."

"Huh?"

Stone reached around and grabbed Scott's hand, then pushed it towards his stiff cock.

"Ahh," the blond said, finally understanding, "you're hard for me again."

"Yes, I fucking am. Let's make the most of it, eh?"

Scott didn't need any more prompting. He moved his hand back to Stone's hip, then used his grip for leverage as he began to piston in and out of his arse. The air was filled with groans as both men voiced their pleasure.

Stone pushed back as Scott thrust forward, and they got into a fast and furious rhythm, resulting in intense stimulation of Stone's prostate gland. He looked down at his rigid prick, which was leaking copious amounts of precum. He was going to come again—and soon. He voiced his thought to Scott, then let out a yelp as the other man began to fuck him even faster—he hadn't thought it possible. But then he hadn't been fucked by a guy as physically fit as Scott before.

He squeezed his eyes shut and braced himself against the rock as Scott pounded them towards climax. Scott came first, digging his fingers so tightly into Stone's hips it would probably leave bruises, and swearing and grunting as his cock spurted hot cum into Stone's back passage.

Stone followed close behind. He'd held out for as long as possible, but the power with which the blond had thrust into him, and the feeling of the thick cock twitching inside him, filling him with cum, sent him over the edge. His own cock leapt, eagerly spilling its release all over the ground as Scott's prick continued to slide against his G-spot. He cried out, then shuddered.

After a minute or two, Scott moved his hands from Stone's hips, only to wrap them around his torso and give him a quick squeeze before stepping away, his softening cock slipping from Stone's arse as he did so.

"Fuck me," Stone said, straightening slowly, his legs wobbly, "that was..." He turned to see Scott wearing an out-of-it facial expression. He remained motionless for a couple of seconds, looking at Stone, before shaking his head and grinning.

"Um, yeah. 'Fuck me' pretty much covers it."

"Come here." Unwilling to trust his unsteady legs, Stone sat on the rock, uncaring of his still half-naked status, and opened his arms. His heart beat faster as Scott approached him willingly. They curled up together on the chilly rock, hardly noticing the cold as their bodies were still so hot.

Scott tilted his head up from its position on Stone's chest and grinned, before stretching up and pressing a kiss to the other man's lips. "I can't believe we just did that."

Stone smiled back, scrubbing his uninjured hand across Scott's hair. "In what way? In that it was me, or that it was here, now?"

"Both, really. I've thought you were hot for ages, but I had no idea you were bi. After I found out, I was so happy and excited I pretty much forgot where we were, much less the fact we were meant to be working!"

"Same here. Weird, eh? But good weird."

"Oh yes, definitely good weird." With that, Scott laid his head back on Stone's chest and they lay in a companionable silence for a while. It was only then Stone realised it had stopped raining. He'd been so in the moment when he and Scott had been fucking that the weather had hardly registered. But now the fact they were damp and cold started to bother him, and he decided that after another minute they'd get up and dressed. Just another minute...

Suddenly, a sound made them sit up and pay attention. A helicopter.

Exchanging a look of horror, they jumped up. They scrambled into their uniforms as fast as possible, making themselves decent and slightly less guilty-looking. And not a moment too soon. Just as they hauled their bags onto their backs and climbed out of the ditch, the chopper emerged from the clouds and began to descend.

The men moved towards the spot where it was coming into land without a word. There was nothing they could say—certainly not with their colleagues so close by. They may not be able to hear over the noise of the aircraft's rotor blades, but they might be able to lip read. Or assess their body language.

Stone shook his head. No, it was better this way. The conversation they needed to have was not one to be rushed or overheard. He still wasn't one hundred per cent sure how Scott felt, but given his actions after they'd had sex, he suspected the other man didn't want it to be a one-off, either.

Suddenly, the idea of being stuck on future exercises with Scott didn't seem so bad, after all. Especially if they were alone. He'd definitely be adding a bottle of lube to his pack in the future, just in case.

Garden of Eden
Chapter One

As Dale approached the club, with its two burly and slightly threatening-looking doormen, he almost turned and walked away. It was just too much, too extreme. Somehow, though, he forced himself to put one foot in front of the other and continue right to the door, then, with a nervous smile at the bouncers, head inside. He paid his cover charge and declined the offer to put his coat in the cloakroom. There was every chance he was going to chicken out at some point this evening, so he didn't want to risk running off, only to realise he'd left his coat behind. Especially since said garment contained his car and house keys, his phone, his wallet...

Plus it helped him hide a little. It covered him from neck—chin if he pulled up the collar—to ankle, secreting his black jeans, black T-shirt and the skinny body beneath them. All anyone could really see were his shock of black hair, his piercing green eyes ringed with eyeliner, fine bone structure and, right down there, his black platform shoes. Dale was a Goth, and proud of it. He got it, understood it, therefore he could deal with it.

What confused him, though, what he *didn't* get, were the urges, the dark thoughts that had led him on his journey to Garden of Eden, his local BDSM club. He'd almost died of embarrassment when he'd searched online to find it and hoped to God no one would ever work out how to check his deleted browser history.

It was a double whammy, really, the fact that he, a twenty-one-year-old virgin, wanted not only to be dominated, but to be dominated—and fucked—by a *man*. He'd taken some time to come to his conclusions, hence the fact he was twenty-one and still had his cherry. He'd never been one for hasty decisions.

And now he was here, at Garden of Eden, to do something about his desires. Of course, he could have gone on the internet, filled in a profile, listed his wants, his preferences, his experience—well, lack of it—but he hadn't wanted to do that. So many people online were not truthful. They hid behind their screens, their keyboards, pretending to be something they weren't. Dale wanted something real, something honest, and he believed the best way to get that was to meet people, people with his desires, face to face. That way he could assess their body language, their words. It wasn't a perfect system, but lying is so much more difficult in the flesh.

He wanted transparency, and he really hoped he would get it in this place. Even if he didn't, though, he was confident he would at least get an education.

He headed through the busy club, squeezing past people dancing, talking, or in much more intimate positions. No one here was too full on—there was lots of kissing, some groping, and a man being led around on a lead, but it was all pretty mild. The research he'd done online had told him that the more hardcore action took place in private rooms. All clubs were different, naturally, but many had rooms with varying equipment in each, catering to the specific needs of the patrons. He figured it would take some time to figure out his *own* specific needs, but perhaps if he managed to find a Master, he would help Dale to work all that out. He hoped so, anyway.

Eventually he reached the bar, where a shaven-headed guy in obscenely tight trousers and a tucked-in, unbuttoned shirt that flashed his entire chest was shaking up a cocktail. He gave a short nod to Dale to acknowledge he'd seen him, then moved back over to the customer he'd been taking care of and served them their drink. He popped a straw into the glass, then took the customer's money with a broad grin. As soon as he'd given the cocktail purchaser their change, the barman headed straight over to Dale.

"Hey, sweet cheeks, welcome to Garden of Eden. What can I get you, first timer?"

Dale couldn't think of how to respond. Was the barman flirting with him, coming on to him, or merely being polite? Perhaps he was a massive flirt and chatted up everyone, men and women alike. And how the hell did he know it was Dale's first time at the club? He couldn't possibly be on shift every single night and recognise every single face he saw.

He cleared his throat. "Hey… you. Thanks. I'll have a Diet Coke. And how do you know it's my first time here?"

The man grabbed a glass and began to pour the drink. "It's written all over your face, sweet cheeks. You look like you don't know whether to jump right in to the action or to run away as fast as your legs will carry you."

His bluntness, his honesty, yanked a laugh from Dale's mouth. "You're very perceptive. And absolutely right. I'm a total newbie to this kind of thing, so I'm hoping everyone will be gentle with me."

The man placed Dale's drink on the bar and popped a straw

into the fizzing liquid. Then he rested his elbows either side of the glass and looked at Dale seriously. "You've come to the right place. This club is so much safer than meeting a stranger online or something. There's a ton of security here, though you'd never know it, and nothing will happen to you unless you want it to. The clientele has respect. But you will need to be a little careful. Once the Doms find out you're a newbie, they'll be climbing over one another to get to you. You're a rare, and hot, commodity." He pushed the glass forward. "On me, babe."

"T-thanks," Dale replied, taking a sip of the fizz as he mulled over the man's words. "Look, I know you're busy, but can I just ask one more question?"

Mr. Tight Trousers inclined his head.

"What exactly is a Dom?" He'd looked it up online, of course, but seeing a description in black and white wasn't the same as a verbal explanation.

The other man laughed, but not in a nasty way. "Wow, you really do have a lot to learn. Well, it's short for Dominant, which tells you most of what you need to know. But everyone's different, so that won't mean the same thing for every man. Just keep your eyes and ears open and take things slow. You'll soon get the hang of it."

Dale wrinkled his nose. "How do you know I'm into men?"

The barman let out a screech of laughter, drawing glances from those nearby. "Sweetheart, have you *seen* me? It takes one to know one, though admittedly I don't go for the BDSM element. I'm quite happy with a simple, straightforward fuck, me. So if you're ever in the market for that kind of thing, you know where I am." He winked at Dale, then headed off to serve his next customer.

Backing away from the bar, his mind racing, Dale wondered what the hell to do next. He was none the wiser on what *exactly* a Dom was, but he was determined to stay, to check the place out properly, see if it was what he was looking for. Or, more specifically, see if it could help him to meet the kind of *person* he was looking for. He had a picture in his mind of his ideal man and, no disrespect to him, but it was *not* the guy behind the bar. Not because he was unattractive or anything—far from it—but because of the way he was. Outlandish, camp.

Dale was looking for pretty much the exact opposite of that. Someone quiet, masculine, intense. The strong and silent type, he supposed. Though, naturally, if someone came along that blew his mind but didn't tick those boxes, then to hell with it. He'd follow his heart—or whatever other parts of his body decided to get involved.

Moving over to the edge of the room in order to be the proverbial wallflower, Dale watched what was going on. The way people behaved, the way they reacted to one another. God, he really needed some kind of crash course in BDSM, in relationships, in being gay… everything. He was utterly clueless, and now he was here, he didn't know where to start.

"Hello."

The deep, luscious voice startled him from his thoughts, tore his attention from the centre of the room, where he'd been watching the guy on the lead and his PVC-clad Mistress. It was no surprise— the voice alone was enough to bring him to his knees; so rich, so delicious, it caressed his ears like melted chocolate pouring across a strawberry.

"H-hi," he eventually choked out, really focusing on the man in front of him for the first time. He'd half expected fate to be cruel and for the owner of the orgasm-inducing voice to be a five feet one, chubby blond. But fate had done no such thing. The man before him was a cliché—an utterly gorgeous cliché. Tall, dark and so good-looking that handsome didn't even come close to covering it, his thick-set frame and smattering of designer stubble fitted his baritone to perfection. Dale was pretty sure he was in love.

Mr. Sex on Legs held out his hand. Dale took it and was a slightly dazed participant in a handshake. When the other man released him, he said, "I'm Al. Pleased to meet you."

"A-al?" He hadn't meant to say that. He'd meant to say his own name, and something pleasant.

"Yes. Or, if you prefer, Alaric Emery Winchester III."

"Dale Smith, pleased to meet you too. Are you posh or something?"

Al laughed. "What gave it away?" He paused. "Yes, I suppose I am. Your first time here?"

Dale nodded, trying hard to calm his nerves and behave like a normal human being, instead of a nervous, gibbering wreck. "Yep. I've never done anything like this before, and I'm not quite sure where to start."

Al leaned a little closer, and Dale got a whiff of his cologne. Something woody, with a touch of spice. Yum. "Well, what exactly is it you're looking for?"

Now Dale had to work extremely hard to make the words come out. His nerves threatened to make them stick in his throat, forcing him to choke on them. "I-I…" He pulled in a deep breath. "I'm a virgin, and I've just recently discovered I'm gay, and also that I'm a… a… submissive."

Al raised his eyebrows, his eyes widened. "Well, that's very interesting, and certainly something you don't hear every day. It seems you've come to the right place."

"Why? Do you know someone here who might be, um, a good match for me?"

"Yes," Al replied, staring so intently at Dale that he felt like a rabbit in the headlights. "Me."

"You?" Dale squeaked. "You mean you're, um… you know?" He wanted to kick himself. Why on earth had he gone all embarrassed about saying the word gay? Or homosexual? He had no problem with the fact Al was a Dom. Even without a scrap of leather or a whip or paddle in his hand, he looked every inch a man who liked to be in charge. But he hadn't had him down as being gay. Which was ridiculous, of course. Camp barman aside, it wasn't always possible to tell a person's sexuality just by looking at them.

"Yes, Dale, I'm gay. And a Dominant. Do you want to go somewhere quieter and talk about this? You're safe with me."

Dale found himself nodding immediately, before his brain even caught up. When it did, he came to the conclusion he should be more cautious, more careful. Instead of saying something to that effect, though, he simply followed when Al turned and walked away. Just because he'd said he'd be safe didn't mean it was true. He could be anyone. His name might not even be Al. Or Alaric, whatever it bloody was. And yet still he put one foot in front of the other as Al led them down a corridor and into a room. He left the door open.

"It's quiet enough in here, isn't it? I've left the door open so you know I'm not dodgy, not trying to hide anything. If you were to scream now, someone would definitely come running to help you. So you've nothing to worry about, I promise."

Chapter Two

Dale didn't know what to say. Which was going to make things awkward, as the whole reason they'd come in here was to talk. He stood just inside the door, shifting from foot to foot.

Al went and sat on what looked like a futon, positioned in the centre of the room. It *was* a futon, Dale decided, only it didn't look like it would ever live in someone's house. Instead of a chintzy pattern, or a trendy one-colour material, it was black leather. But what made it really unsuitable for your average house was the fact the legs of the damn thing were covered in scary-looking silver spikes. Basically, it was right at home in a BDSM club. Even so, it looked dangerous to Dale—what if someone tripped and impaled themselves on it?

"Hey," Al said, waving to get Dale's attention. "Come sit here. I won't bite. Not unless you ask me to." He grinned, and Dale's face heated up so rapidly he thought his head might explode.

He shuffled over to the futon and sat on it—not so far away from Al that it looked as though he was trying to avoid him, but not too close, either. He was already distracted by the other man's presence. Any more of that and he wouldn't have a single sensible thing to say, and their chat would be pretty one-sided.

"So," Al said gently, turning to face Dale. "You only just realised you're gay, and that you're a submissive. And now you're here. It must all be pretty overwhelming?" His expression was open, welcoming. Kind.

Dale frowned. This was not at all what he'd been expecting from a Dom. Weren't they supposed to be bossy, mean, whip your arse until it was purple? He shook his head. No, he was generalising. Just as not every gay man was camp, not every Dom was mean, and into pain. He really hoped Al wasn't into pain. Although he hadn't actually done *anything* remotely sexual with anyone—beyond kissing a couple of girls and finding he wasn't that impressed—or anything submissive, he knew, deep down, that he wasn't into pain. He'd probably give it a go, just to be sure, but he was ninety-nine-point-nine percent convinced he wouldn't like it. It was the power play element that interested him.

To him, the part of submission which attracted him the most was having the pressure of making decisions removed. Someone else would tell him what to do to them, or tie him up, cuff him or whatever, and do what they wanted to him. He could relax—mentally, of course; he wasn't sure it was at all relaxing physically—and let his Dom take care of the sexual pleasure element. The other person would do all of the thinking, all of the decision-making, and he'd be free to just concentrate on doing as he was told. There was the small matter of him still being a virgin, but he hoped that losing his cherry would be part of the overall experience. He didn't want it to be a big deal, an issue, he just wanted the right man to come along and take care of everything.

Was that man Al? It seemed incredible that the very first time he'd visited a club, the first time he'd done anything about his desires other than research on the internet, he'd met someone who could potentially fit the bill. It seemed too good to be true, which was why he was holding back, why he wasn't jumping into Al's arms and begging him to have his wicked way with him. He didn't want to get hurt, to get tossed aside like rubbish once he'd been used.

Plus, there was the small matter he hadn't dared voice, barely even to himself. He didn't just want a Dom. He wanted love. Maybe it was silly, idealistic, but he only wanted to give himself to someone when there was more between them than just physical attraction.

He realised Al was staring at him. Hardly surprising, given the man had asked him a question, and instead of replying he'd retreated into his own head. "S-sorry. Yes, I guess I am overwhelmed. I've just got so much stuff going through my mind, I don't know where to start."

Al shifted along the futon, closer to him, then took his hand. "Well, there's no rush. No rush to say anything, no rush to do anything. You'll get absolutely no pressure from me, and if you decide you don't want to talk to me or do anything with me, just tell me, and I'll back off. Will you promise me one thing, though?"

Dale met Al's eyes. "What?"

"Promise me that if you don't want me to be your Dom, that you'll be careful finding someone else. If it becomes general knowledge that you're a virgin, both sexually and submissively, you'll get lots of men making you offers. But, as in any type of relationship, straight, lesbian, bisexual, vanilla, kinky, not everyone is respectful or truthful. I don't think you'll have any trouble in here as it's a good club, but please, just take care of yourself."

Dale thought he'd fallen in love there and then. Really and truly, this time. A sexy, kind, intelligent man was talking to him about all these things, and emphasising that he had no intention of putting any pressure on him? It was like he was wrapping Dale up in cotton wool or something. It should have been annoying, patronising, made him feel like a child, but it didn't. It just felt as though he'd met a genuinely wonderful man who was offering him all of the things he wanted most.

"N-no, it's okay. I like you, Al, and I'd like to get to know you better. Before we, um, do anything."

"Wonderful." Al clapped his hands, seeming genuinely delighted. "Okay, well how about we go on a date, then? I don't mean right now, of course. Another night, whenever suits you."

Dale fidgeted. A date? How exactly did that work when it was two men doing the dating?

"Dale," Al said gently, "what's the matter? What did I say?"

"Nothing. It's just…"

"Go on, you can tell me."

"I know. It's just a bit awkward. I was wondering, what exactly happens when two men go on a date? I know times have changed and all that, but don't people stare?"

Al laughed. "Bless you, you really are having a hard time of this, aren't you? Well, as long as you want me around, I'll do what I can to help you, make things easier for you. To answer your question, no, they don't. Unless we start holding hands or kissing across the table, how would people even know we were gay? We could be friends, brothers, business associates. Hell, with our age difference, we could even be father and son."

Dale snapped his head up and looked at Al. *Really* looked at him. The tiny lines around his eyes, on his forehead, the handful of grey hairs at his temples. Christ, up until now he hadn't even thought about there being an age difference between them. Possibly because he felt older than he was. Despite his sexual inexperience, he was mature in other ways. But it seemed he had indeed got himself a sugar daddy. And a dominant one, at that. "Yes, okay. I'd love to go on a date with you."

"Great. Name a time and a place and I'll get it all organised."

There he was again, being so different to what Dale had expected. He'd have thought that *Al* would be the one naming the time and the place, then expecting Dale to turn up. He shrugged. Whatever. He'd have to throw all his preconceptions out of the window and start afresh, learn things as they happened, and see how things progressed between the two of them.

One thing he was pretty sure of, though, was that he'd be losing his cherry—in both senses of the word—to Al. Soon.

"Well," he said with a smile, "I'm busy tomorrow, but I could do the evening after."

"The evening? Where will you be in the day?"

"University. I'm a student."

"Oh." That shut Al up for a good few seconds. "God, you really are young, aren't you? I'm beginning to think I should ask for some identification to make sure I'm not breaking any laws."

Dale bristled. "I can't help my age, Al. But I can assure you, I'm twenty-one. If you want to see my driving license…"

Al waved his hands dismissively. "No, no, I believe you. It's fine. Okay, the day after tomorrow is superb. Do you know where you want to go?"

The younger man shook his head. "No. I've never been on a date. I don't really know where people go, what they do."

"Would you like for me to choose somewhere?"

"Yes, please. And let me know the dress code. Though I might have to buy something more suitable." He gestured at his all-black outfit.

Al shook his head. "No, you won't. I'll choose somewhere where you'll look fine just as you dress naturally. How you're comfortable. You wear whatever you like, and if they don't like it, then they won't get our custom, will they?"

Dale couldn't help it—he let out a bark of laughter. "You're very determined, aren't you? Do you like my Goth get up or something? Does it get you going?"

"No." He shook his head. "I mean, yes. No. Argh. Let me start again. Yes, I'm determined. Yes, I like your Goth get up. But it doesn't get me going, as such. *You* get me going, Dale. You as a whole. Not your black coat, not your makeup—the whole of you. And how you dress is a part of you, a part of your personality, your life, and I wouldn't dream of changing it."

"You're seriously trying to impress me, aren't you?" He gave a wry grin.

Al sighed. "Yes, of course. But that's not why I'm saying it. I'm saying it because I mean it. Are you always so sceptical?"

"Pretty much. Ever since I became a teenager, I've dressed like this. And, apart from the other kids at school who were Goth, everyone took the piss out of me. Cool kids, even the not-so-cool kids, my teachers, my parents—"

"Your *parents* took the piss out of you?"

"No, not exactly. And nor did my teachers. Not really. They just showed their displeasure, the fact that they didn't agree with my look, that they didn't get it. Uni's different, somehow. Maybe it's because the students are older, everything's so much more laid back—everyone has their quirks and they're accepted. One of my lecturers looks like a hippie, for God's sake!"

Al smirked. "Now you sound like *you're* being judgmental."

"No, no I'm not. I'm not judging him—I was just emphasising that at uni, it's okay to look, to behave—within reason—however you like."

"Sounds like a great place to be."

Dale nodded emphatically. "It is. I feel happier there than I ever was in my previous education."

"I'm glad to hear it. What are you studying?"

"English and English Literature."

"And you're enjoying that? Doing well?"

"Yes. And, uh, why?"

"Why, what?"

"Why do you want to know if I'm doing well?"

Al frowned. "I'm making conversation. Getting to know you. That all right?"

Dale blushed. "Sorry. Yes, of course. And yeah, I'm doing good. So, what about you? What do you do?"

Chapter Three

Dale tugged at his black shirt, then smoothed his clammy hands down his black trousers. He felt okay dressed like this, even without makeup. What was making him nervous was the fact he was on a date—or was about to be, anyway.

Glancing at his reflection in the restaurant window, he took a deep breath and headed for the door. He had no idea what he was doing, but Al had promised to guide him through it, through anything he needed him to.

Passing into the air-conditioned corridor, then through to the main room and the maitre d's podium, he resisted the temptation to look around and see if Al was here already. Even if he wasn't, he'd be here soon, he was sure of it.

"Can I help you, sir?" The maitre d' said without cracking a smile.

"Yes, please. I'm Dale Smith. I'm here to meet Mr. Winchester. Alaric Winchester."

The man's slightly haughty attitude changed immediately. He glanced down at the list on his podium, then straightened, smiled—it was instantly clear he didn't do *that* very often—gave a tiny bow, and said, "Certainly, sir. I'll take you to your table right away. Mr. Winchester is expecting you."

Dale had to bite back a grin as he fell into step behind the man. It was funny how he'd gone from indifferent to ingratiating with the mere mention of Al's name. It seemed he really was keeping important company. A flash of worry bolted through him at the thought. What the hell *was* Alaric Emery Winchester the Third doing with him, plain old Dale Smith? Was it the virgin thing? Making him a rare commodity, even to someone whose name made him sound like nobility? Someone who could have anyone, anything, he wanted?

He didn't even realise they'd reached the table until Al spoke. "What on earth's the matter, Dale? You look like you've seen a ghost. Jeeves, can we get some water, please?"

The man backed away with another little bow.

Dale couldn't help but grin. "Jeeves? Seriously?"

Al shrugged. "Probably not. I've been calling him that since the first time I came here, and it seems to have stuck. Everyone calls him that now. Poor guy probably hates me. Please, sit down."

He did as he was asked, sliding into the booth opposite Al. Looking around at his surroundings, he realised they were so secluded, so far from any other diners that it felt like they had the place to themselves. He finally shifted his gaze onto his date. "I can't imagine anyone hating you."

"Aw, shucks. Thank you. I'm sure lots of people do. But never mind them. Are you going to tell me what had you looking so worried just then?"

"Nothing, really, just nerves. This is my first date, remember."

"Of course." Al seemed satisfied with his answer. "Well, I'll do everything I can to make sure you relax and enjoy yourself. I really wish you'd let me pick you up from home. You'd have loved the limousine."

Dale raised his eyebrows. He'd wondered if accepting a lift

would have meant a ride in a limo. He'd refused, partly because he didn't want a flash car attracting attention, and partly because his parents would have insisted on meeting his date if 'she'd' come to their house. He hadn't quite got around to telling them he was gay, yet. They'd only just started to accept the way he dressed, the fact he wore makeup and painted his nails. They probably wouldn't be surprised, though—they'd asked so many times in the past if his style choices were a sign of his sexuality. Though not so subtly. He'd just sighed, rolled his eyes and refused to dignify their questions with answers. So, having never confirmed nor denied it, they'd just believe they'd been right all along—even though Dale had only just come to the conclusion himself.

Al's voice broke into his thoughts. "You're doing it again. Looking worried."

"What? Oh, sorry. Just thinking how much of a stir a man arriving in a limo would have caused at my house."

"Oh, yes. Of course. I'm sorry, I never thought. Forgive me?"

"There's nothing to forgive. Just help me prepare to tell my parents I'm gay, okay?"

"I'll be there, if you like."

Dale coughed, an image of his dad and Al squaring up to each other flitting through his mind. "No, no, that won't be necessary."

Just then, Jeeves arrived with a carafe of iced water and two crystal glasses. "Your waiter will be along shortly to take your drinks orders and give you menus."

"Thank you, Jeeves," Al said.

The man gave a nod, his face not registering even the faintest flicker of irritation, then left.

Al turned to Dale, grinning. "He probably spits in my food." He picked up the carafe and filled the two glasses. His smile widening at Dale's horrified expression, he continued, "So, how do you like this place so far? Nice, huh?"

The younger man smiled politely. "Yeah, I guess."

"You guess? This is the most expensive place in town. The chef has three Michelin stars."

Dale raised an eyebrow. "I don't doubt it, but I'd have been more than happy with pub grub. You don't have to try so hard. Just let me get to know you, make me laugh, have fun with me, and we'll be just fine." He was glad the restaurant provided such a quiet, private corner, where the two of them could have this conversation without fear of being overheard.

Al looked abashed. "Okay, noted. I'll take you to bloody McDonald's if it's what you want. You want to leave? We don't have to stay here if you don't want to."

"No," Dale said decisively, "this is fine. Lovely. It was just a note for future reference."

"Fair enough. So, what do you want to drink? Wine, champagne, beer? Whatever you like." He took a sip of the water, and Dale did the same, appreciative of the chilly liquid.

"I'm not much of a drinker, I must confess. But I'd like a small glass of wine, if that's all right? What are you having?"

"I'll have the same as you. What wine do you want? Red,

white, Rose? I'll call the sommelier over."

"I dunno. It all tastes the same to me."

Al laughed, slapping the table so hard it made Dale jump. "Christ, you're a philistine!"

"No," Dale snapped, whacking both his hands down on the table, "I'm just not posh. I'm not anyone-the-fucking-third. I'm just me, Dale Smith. And it's definitely Smith, not Smythe, so if you don't like it, maybe I should leave."

He glared at Al, who now looked thoroughly upset. He made to reach out and take Dale's hand, then thought better of it. "Please don't go. I'm really sorry. I guess I'm nervous, too, and it's making me say stupid things. God, I'm such an idiot." He put his head in his hands, then ran his fingers through his hair, making it stand on end.

Dale didn't reply. He wasn't going to say it was okay, because it really wasn't. He'd had the piss taken out of him for years. He wasn't about to get into a relationship with someone who did it, too. That would make *him* the idiot.

The waiter arrived, poised to take their order. Al asked for the sommelier. The waiter nodded and left again. He came back a few seconds later with their menus. "So you can decide on your wine." And he was gone again.

The two men sat in silence for a minute or two, flipping through their respective menus. Eventually, Al spoke. "Are you staying, Dale?" Hope shone in his eyes.

Dale tried to glare at him again, and failed miserably. So he'd fucked up—so what? He was only human. He'd let it slide this time, as they were both nervous. But if it happened again—tonight or otherwise—he was out of there. "Yes, I'll stay. So, we have to choose what we want so we can have the 'right' wine to go with it, yes?"

"Yes." Al said nothing else. No further comment, no smirk. Apparently he'd learned his lesson and wouldn't let his nerves manifest in that way again.

For the second time, Dale wondered at the power he held over Al. They weren't even playing together, or 'scening' as he'd seen it called on various websites, and yet he felt there were power plays going on. The odd thing was *he* seemed to be the one in charge. It felt backwards to him, but then he had a lot to learn. An awful lot, apparently.

He looked at the menu again, then made his decision. "Okay, I'll have the pâté, the chateaubriand, and the crème brûlée, please."

"Sounds great. So bloody great that I'm going to have the same. Well, beef is best complemented by a red wine. And that's where this gentleman," he indicated the smartly-dressed man approaching their booth, "comes in."

The sommelier gave them a nod as he reached them, then politely enquired, "What are you having for dinner, gentlemen?"

Al filled him in, and he nodded thoughtfully, stared into space for a couple of seconds, then reeled off a list of wines. "If you let me know if you like sweet or dry wine, and so on, I can narrow down your choices considerably."

Al glanced over to Dale, who shrugged helplessly. Smirking a little, he turned back to the sommelier. "We'll go for a sweet wine, please."

A couple more exchanges later, and between them, Al and the wine expert had made a decision. With another nod, he went to collect a bottle of their chosen drink. A few minutes later he was back, and pouring a drop into a glass for Al to taste. Dale noticed Al sniffed the liquid, too. He really had no idea what was going on, so he just went with the flow, smiling politely when the sommelier poured some of the reddish-purple liquid into his glass.

"All right?" Al asked once they were alone.

Dale nodded. "A little confused and overwhelmed, but I'll get over it."

"It is a bit weird in these places, I admit. There's so much pomp and ceremony, so many choices to make. I think your idea of pub grub is excellent. If you'll agree to another date with me, that's what we'll do. Steak and ale pie with a pint of beer sounds like heaven to me."

They both laughed, and Dale realised he was the most relaxed he'd been all evening. Yes, they'd had ups and downs, but he was rapidly getting used to Al and his ways, not to mention the fact he was on a date with a man. Maybe by the end of the night he'd feel like taking things further. Only time would tell.

Chapter Four

As Dale and Al exited the restaurant, the tension was palpable. They'd chatted and laughed their way through three courses, an undercurrent of attraction running throughout. Now was the time to either call it a night, or… not.

"Can I drive you home? I'll drop you round the corner, if you like." His smile, visible in the dim light from the restaurant sign, was genuine, not mocking.

"Thanks," Dale replied, returning the grin, "but I came in my car."

"Oh." Al's shoulders sagged, and Dale felt a pull in both his chest and nether regions. The other man brightened a little, and asked, "Well, how about a nightcap? I've got soft drinks—if you can still call that a nightcap."

The pulling sensation became an ache. Dale's heart and groin were screaming a resounding yes, but his head was screaming an equally loud no. "Um, I'm not sure I should."

"Why? I promise there won't be any funny business. Unless you want there to be, obviously."

"That's what I'm worried about." He sighed. "I'm worried about taking things too fast—skipping right past the getting to know each other part and jumping into bed. Or wherever. Christ, do you have a dungeon?" He hadn't meant to say the last part, but it was too late. He gave a sheepish grin.

Al laughed. "No, I don't have a dungeon. I live in a flat, for starters, so there's only one floor. And even if I didn't, I wouldn't have a dungeon. I'm not into all that, into pain, restraints, equipment.

I like to keep things simple, and really test my submissives by making them do my bidding without any assistance."

"Oh!" The word was loud and high-pitched, rapidly followed by a nervous giggle. "Well, uh, that's good, I guess. Obviously I can't be totally sure, but I don't think I'm into pain either."

The older man nodded carefully. "There's nothing stopping us trying it if you ever feel the need. But back to the other part of what you said, about taking things too fast, I'm afraid I can't promise anything. I will certainly not initiate anything or force you, but if you make any moves then I doubt very much I'll be able to refuse you." He took a deep breath, ran his fingers through his hair. "Can I be honest with you?"

Dale nodded, his heart thumping. God, what was he going to say now?

"It's insane, totally unhinged, off the wall, any other word for crazy you can think of. But it's true. Dale… I want you. Really fucking want you. More than I've ever wanted anyone before. And I don't just mean for sex, or submission. Or both. You challenge me, somehow, complicate things and yet make them so simple. Fuck, I'm not even making any sense. But, well… fuck it. Dale, I have feelings for you, all right? I'm not saying it's love, because I don't believe in love at first sight and all that, but I strongly suspect that if we continue seeing each other, things will definitely go in that direction. For me, at least." Al fiddled with his hair again, shifted his weight from one foot to the other, looked around, then finally moved his gaze back to Dale. "For God's sake, say something."

Dale snorted. "What the fuck am I supposed to say to that?"

He paused. "I know what you're getting at, though. I... I feel the same. God, how is this happening? We've only met twice. And we only had a small glass of wine each, so we're not drunk. Is this just lust, though? Our hormones taking control of our minds?"

Al shook his head. "Absolutely not. Not for me, anyway. I've been around a lot longer than you, and I know the difference between love and lust. In my own head, anyway. Obviously I can't speak for you, and I would never want to, either." He let out a shaky breath. "I tell you what, shall we sleep on this? Part ways now and see how we feel in the morning?"

"Yes, I like that idea." Dale smiled and shook his head incredulously. "God, you're just perfect in every way, aren't you? Are you sure you're not a dream?"

"No, I'm not perfect, Dale. Far from it. But I'm glad you think so. It's a good sign. Okay, well, where's your car?"

Dale pointed across the street. "There."

"Oh. Well, I'll just wait here until you're safely inside, then. I'll buzz my driver." He pulled his phone from his pocket, tapped the screen a few times, then put it away.

Dale nodded. "Yeah, uh, okay. Thanks for a lovely evening. Bye." He didn't know what the fuck to do next, what the etiquette was, so he turned abruptly and walked away, checking the road for traffic before crossing to his car. He retrieved his keys from his pocket, and was just about to press the button to unlock the doors when he had a change of heart. A maelstrom of thoughts bombarded his mind.

Fuck being in love. He had to lose his cherry—in all

respects—at some point, didn't he? So why not lose it with a gorgeous, sexy, lovely, kind guy whom he had feelings for, however sudden and irrational? Even if Al tired of him within days, weeks, he'd have had a good time, with a man he knew would take care of him. Then he'd be more experienced, and perhaps possess a slightly harder heart for the next time a Dom came along.

Fuck it. You only live once. He turned and dashed back across the road, and caught Al just as he was about to step into the limousine. "Hey, wait. Is it okay if I change my mind?"

Al looked as though he was trying to stop a huge grin appearing on his face, and failed miserably. Adorable wrinkles at the corners of his eyes and his lips stretching almost from ear to ear reassured Dale that he'd made the right decision. Whatever happened afterwards, he was about to have the best night of his life.

"Of course," Al said, stepping back and gesturing into the vehicle. "I'd be absolutely delighted."

"No, it's okay. I'll follow in my car. I don't want to leave it here."

"Fair enough. I'd offer to ride with you, but that's probably not a good idea."

Dale shook his head. "You're right. Give me a minute, then, and I'll follow you."

"Will do."

Dale made his way back to his car and clambered in, then started the engine and put on his seatbelt. He looked across the road; the limousine was indicating to pull out, so he flicked on his own indicator and fell in behind it when it started to move. It was a bit weird to be actively tailing a car, but his reasons were good, and now he'd made the decision, he had no intention of going back on it. He heaved a sigh of relief. A weight had been lifted. It appeared the anticipation, the not knowing, had been playing on his mind. But now he knew where he was going and, more importantly, why. Even though he didn't know exactly what was going to happen once he got to Al's place, he didn't mind. The older man had managed to earn his trust in a very short amount of time, and he just hoped it wouldn't be abused.

After ten minutes or so, Al's car pulled into a cul-de-sac, drove all the way to the end, then paused as a set of iron gates opened to admit it. The limo drove smoothly through them, and Dale waited, not knowing what to do next. Should he follow, or should he find somewhere to park out on the street?

His question was answered when Al suddenly came jogging over to him. Dale opened the car window.

"Just head straight through the gates, they'll close automatically behind you. Then head over to the left and you'll see a bunch of parking spaces marked with a 'V'—for visitors. Just park there, and I'll wait for you by the front door."

He pointed over to a large building, lit up by street lamps and security lights. It was enormous—some kind of converted factory, it looked like. "Okay, see you in a mo." He found a space, parked up, locked the car, then headed to the building. As promised, Al stood by the front door.

"Hey," he said. "Ready?"

"As I'll ever be." Dale bit his lip, silently punishing himself for the stupid clichéd response. Al didn't seem to notice. He'd already turned and punched a code into a keypad mounted on the wall. A buzzing sound began, and Al pushed the door open, walked through and held it open for Dale.

"I'm on the top floor, so I think we'll use the lift."

"Good plan." Of course he was on the top floor. He probably had the entire top floor, a full-on penthouse. Dale kept quiet, not wanting to ruin the mood. They moved over to the lift, where Al pressed the button, and they waited for it to come down to the ground floor. They stepped in together once the doors opened. Dale leaned on the wall and watched as Al entered a code into another keypad, then pressed the button for the sixth floor. Damn, it really was a penthouse—otherwise surely he'd have just pressed the floor button.

They remained silent as the steel box transported them to their destination.

Dale had no idea what to expect as the ping rang out and the doors parted, but he wasn't exactly surprised. The place was *huge*. At first glance it looked modern, clean, tidy and *expensive*.

"Wow," was all he had to say.

Al laughed. "Yeah, most people have that reaction. I've lived here five years and even I still think it's cool. Come on in."

Dale stepped out of the lift after Al, his eyes wide as he took in even more of the beautiful home. There was lots of cream and white, with occasional splashes of vivid colour. There wasn't a St. Andrew's Cross to be seen, either. It seemed Al really did keep his sexual preferences confined to the bedroom. Or wherever—it certainly wasn't apparent in this portion of the apartment. But then, why would it be? He shook his head at his own silliness.

"Do you like it?" Al asked.

"Yes, it's gorgeous. A million miles away from my tiny bedroom at my parents' house. This is really, really beautiful, and I'm wildly jealous."

The older man smiled. "Well, you're welcome here any time. Now, can I get you anything? A drink? Something to eat?"

"Something to eat? You're kidding, right? We just ate a three-course meal!"

"What can I say, I have a fast metabolism. A drink, then?"

"A Diet Coke would be great, thanks."

Al entered the kitchen area of the mostly open-plan apartment and grabbed a bottle from the fridge, then filled two glasses. He came back to where Dale still stood and passed him the drink. "Want to sit down?" He gestured to the chocolate-coloured sofa.

"No," Dale said abruptly, putting his glass down on a nearby table. "No, I don't. I want you to show me your bedroom."

"Uh, okay." Al put his own drink down and led the way to a door in the far corner of the space.

Dale followed, slightly dazed. Where on earth had that sudden outburst come from? The overwhelming need to see Al's bedroom had taken him over, apparently.

Perhaps more accurately, he wanted to do what people did in bedrooms. He wanted the anticipation over and done with, the thinking, wondering, wishing. The fucking waiting. Dale Smith wanted to submit to, and have sex with, Alaric Emery Winchester the Third, and fast.

He moved quickly into the bedroom behind Al, barely giving the room a glance. Instead, he slipped his arms around the other man's waist and squeezed.

"Hey," Al said gently, turning in his arms, his brow creased. "What are you doing?"

"What do you think? I want you, Al. And I don't want to wait. Even if it's only one time with you and you get bored of me, I don't care. I want to submit to you, have sex with you, come with you."

Al's jaw almost hit the floor. "What? You think I'll get bored of you?"

"Not necessarily. I hope you won't."

"That's pretty bloody unlikely. Now stop being so damn paranoid and tell me again that you want me."

"I want you."

His eyebrows lifted. "Really? Now, tonight? This is your last chance to change your mind. If you consent, then I'm in charge until we leave this bedroom. But I can promise you one thing, I'll never hurt you."

Chapter Five

Instead of replying, Dale pulled Al more tightly to him and kissed him. It was closed-mouth for barely a second, then both men parted their lips, eager for more. Al put his arms around Dale's neck as their tongues battled, danced, explored. The younger man was blissed-out and overwhelmed all at once. Sensations battered him—arousal, ecstasy, a frisson of danger as Al's stubble brushed against his skin, reminding him that their union would not be all sweetness and light. It would be new, different, exciting and no doubt challenging.

He couldn't wait to get started. He poured everything he felt into the kiss, hoping to say to Al with his lips and tongue everything he couldn't voice. He was on a natural high, he felt good, so damn good. Every nerve ending was alight, every millimetre of skin aching for more; his cock pressing so hard, so insistently against the inside of his boxers and trousers that he thought it might figure out how to undo the zip by itself.

Al's cock was much the same, an iron bar of need pressed against his groin, making him want to drop to his knees and take it in his mouth, worship it, love it. But that would come in time, he knew it would. It had to.

The room was filled with gasps, grunts, moans as their need climbed higher and higher, threatening to spiral out of control. Finally, Al pulled away, sucking in a deep breath. As he did so, his lust-drunk expression morphed into an utterly serious one.

"Take off your clothes."

Dale paused only for a millisecond before doing as he was

commanded. His body registered before his brain how aroused the words had made him. His cock surged. Once naked, he picked up his pile of clothes and placed them on a chair in the corner of the room, then looked back at Al, waiting to see what he would have to do next.

"Kneel."

This time, Dale's response was instantaneous.

"Do you have a safe word?"

"Yes." He didn't know if he was meant to call Al "Sir". He'd read that it wasn't something expected across the board. Every Dom was different. He was sure he'd soon be corrected if he'd got it wrong. "It's 'hobbit'."

The older man raised an eyebrow, but said nothing about it. "Good. Now, I'm going to take off my clothes, and when I have, I want you to get in front of me and suck my cock." He started removing his clothes immediately, and Dale watched, transfixed, as the most perfect body he'd ever seen was revealed to him.

His chest was broad, muscled, hairy, but not too much of either. A tantalising trail of hair led from his belly button into the waistband of his trousers, which he was in the process of removing. They fell to the floor, and Dale drank in the sight of thick, strong-looking legs as the other man bent to pull off his socks, then straightened and slipped off his underwear. He could hardly wait to see his cock. Would it be long, thick, both? Smooth, veiny? Whatever, it was going to be perfect, just like the man it belonged to.

Finally, he saw his soon-to-be lover in all his naked glory. He immediately knew he'd be willing to worship this man in any way he saw fit until his dying day. Lick and suck his cock until he got lockjaw, kneel until he got cramp, fuck and be fucked to the point of exhaustion. He remained distracted for a moment longer, until he looked up and saw Al's expectant expression. It was then he remembered the command.

He shuffled forward as quickly as he could manage, then circled his fingers around Al's cock and immediately closed his mouth over the head. He had no real idea what he was doing, so he proceeded to do what he thought he'd like to have done to him, and hope Al was vocal enough that it was obvious what got him going, and what didn't.

"I know you haven't done this before, so I'll forgive the use of your hand. But in future, you may not use your hands unless I give you express permission."

Dale nodded, then, eager to please, sank his mouth down Al's shaft. The sweet-yet-salty taste of precum glided over his tongue, and he hummed with pleasure as the long, thick dick filled him. It was difficult to stimulate the other man when his mouth was so full, but he experimented with flicks of his tongue, tighter suction with his lips, pulling his cheeks in so they were hollow, and anything else that came to mind.

Al had been fairly quiet to begin with, just the occasional low moan passing his lips. But it seemed he was getting hornier and hornier, as his breathing grew faster and heavier, the occasional expletive popped out and his shaft grew so hot and hard it was like heated steel. Encouraged, Dale carried on, and quickly learned exactly what to do to make Al groan louder, swear more often, and leak more precum onto his waiting tongue.

Dale was in heaven. He'd barely started being Al's submissive, and already he loved it. He was sure there were some things he'd be expected to do in the future that he wouldn't like, or would find difficult, but he knew he'd overcome it. He would do anything to please the older man, anything to make him happy. Their relationship was still in its infancy, but something deep down inside Dale told him Al felt the same way he did—like they were going to be together a very long time. Possibly even a lifetime.

Al grew increasingly out of control. He tangled his fingers in Dale's hair, gripped and yanked hard, sending shards of pleasure slicing through his lover. Jerking his hips, he forced his cock deeper down Dale's throat. Dale did his best to accommodate him, pulling in deep breaths through his nostrils with each thrust, so he could relax his gag reflex and allow the meaty head of Al's cock to penetrate his throat. He sent up a silent thanks to the internet, which was the only reason he knew what deep-throating was, and how he could achieve it.

"Unh, Dale, I'm going to come…"

Dale reached around and gripped Al's arse cheeks, then pulled him harder and faster into his mouth, swirling his tongue wildly and creating as much delicious friction as possible. Perhaps he'd pay for using his hands later, but right now he couldn't get enough of his lover, of his cock, and of the spunk that was now jetting into his mouth, covering his tongue, his teeth, his gums. He licked and sucked at it eagerly, swallowing every last drop.

He felt so wanted, so needed, and somehow so powerful.

Dale was the one on his knees, but Al was the one blaspheming and utterly losing control. It was so good, so heady, that he was sure even the brush of a feather against his own shaft would send him spiralling into his own much-needed climax.

After cleaning every last drop of juice from Al's cock, he gently disentangled himself from him, then sat back on his heels and looked up at his lover's face. He liked what he saw, very much. The other man's flawless skin was flushed, with two high spots of colour on his cheeks. His eyes were wide, his mouth hung open. He looked utterly bowled over, utterly... fucked.

Dale smiled a secret smile. He could get used to this. At the same time, he wanted so much more. To be fucked by his gorgeous Dom, to have him spill his seed inside his arse, for them to rock and sweat together until they were both overcome with pleasure. It sounded like a damn good way to spend the rest of the evening, certainly. But really, he wanted it forever. Somehow, in a ridiculously small space of time, he'd fallen for the tall, dark and dominant older man. He'd fallen under his spell, and he didn't care. Happiness, he decided, was something everyone deserved, and he knew he'd found it here, with Alaric Emery Winchester the Third.

"Hey," Al's voice sounded croaky, breathless. "Get up." The last two words sounded slightly more authoritative, but not much. It didn't matter—Dale did it anyway. Because he wanted to, because he *had* to. There didn't have to be anything formal about their relationship—he'd read about collaring ceremonies and the like—for him to want to serve his Dom. And serve him he would. For as long as he wanted him to.

"Come on," Al continued, "let's go to bed. Just give me five minutes and I'll be ready to go again. Then I'm going to fuck your sweet little arse and watch your face as I do it."

A thrill of decadent pleasure ran through Dale as he scampered across the room and all but flung himself onto the bed.

Al laughed. "You're eager."

"Yes, I am. Right here, right now, I've got everything a man could ever want. And yet, you're still offering me more."

"More sex? More submission? Or something else?" He joined Dale on the bed and pulled the younger man into his arms before stroking the black hair that now stood on end.

"All of the above, I think. But you need to know, I'm willing to take whatever you want to give. A casual relationship, something non-exclusive, whatever…"

"*What*? What are you even *saying*?" He stiffened, moved away from Dale and glared at him across the expanse of bed. His eyes flashed with anger, and Dale had to resist the instinct to shrink away from him. "Why the hell are you undervaluing yourself that way? Saying that you're willing to take whatever I'm willing to give you? You make yourself sound so fucking worthless, Dale, and that makes me angry. You're worth so much more than that…" He heaved a deep breath, then scooted across the bed once more, the majority of his ire seemingly diminished. He cupped Dale's head in his hands and pressed a searing hot kiss to his lips. "You're worth so much more than that to me, Dale Smith. I want everything from you. Submission, sex, exclusivity, love. And I'm willing to give you the same in return. Except for the submission, obviously."

The laugh got caught in Dale's throat. Had he really said *love* in amongst the rest of his speech? "You… love me?"

Al nodded. "I know it's early days, but I'm definitely falling for you, Dale, in a big way. Like I said earlier, I definitely think love is going to happen."

Dale gulped. "I feel exactly the same about you." He paused. "Can I ask you something?"

"Of course."

"Fuck me?"

"Definitely."

With that, Al pushed Dale so he was flat on his back, then retrieved a bottle of lube and a condom from his bedside cabinet. He prepared Dale carefully, lovingly, like he was his finest treasure. Then he rolled the rubber down his once-again stiff shaft, covered it with more lube, and pressed himself up against Dale's tight pucker.

"Ready?" he whispered.

"Ready," Dale replied with a grin. And he was. So fucking ready to give himself to his Dom fully. To lose his final cherry. Submission and sex—he'd willingly given them to a man older than him, richer than him, posher than him. And it didn't matter. When it came down to it, they were just two men with complementary desires. And they fitted together perfectly.

Fired Up

Lucas Hartley grabbed his helmet and equipment and jumped out of the fire truck. The helmet wasn't a requirement to go and fit smoke detectors, but if the house had kids, it was pretty much a necessity. He'd yet to come across a rug-rat who didn't ask Lucas to put his fireman's helmet on, then take it off so *they* could try it on. He quite liked kids, so it was nice to see their little grinning faces, to make their day. Plus, if they were a handful, he could use the helmet as bribery to make them behave while he fitted the detectors and ran through a comprehensive fire safety discussion with a responsible adult. It never failed.

The downside, however, was that the whole fireman-in-uniform thing often got the responsible adults of the female persuasion all hot under the collar. For most guys, this wouldn't be a problem. After all, a little flirtation here and there was good for the ego. But for Lucas, it was a drag—why couldn't there be a single dad somewhere who was gay and needed a smoke detector fitting? Sadly, it just never seemed to work out that way.

Sighing, Lucas slammed the door on the mocking comments of his colleagues, who'd opted to stay in the truck. It only took one person to do the job in question, and today Lucas had drawn the short straw—literally. The others would no doubt chill out, chat and use their phones to text, mess around on Facebook, or play games until he was done, or an emergency came in. Whatever was first.

Rolling his eyes, he let out another heavy breath, then rearranged his face into a smile. No point taking his grumpiness out on the homeowner. He strode up to the door, put his equipment down, then grasped the knocker and gave it a firm tap against the wood. After a short pause, he heard the unmistakable sound of a key turning in a lock, and the door was opened a little. A woman's face appeared in the gap. She looked him up and down, then peered around him to the large red truck parked at the end of her driveway.

Apparently satisfied he wasn't a cold caller, she opened the door wider. "Hello," she said, smiling. "Come on in."

"Thanks." Lucas picked up his gear and moved into the hallway, then waited while the woman shut the door.

After doing so, she indicated he should head through an open doorway into the living room. Lucas entered the room, and was just about to ask the woman—Mrs. Judd, according to his paperwork—if she knew where she wanted the detectors fitting, when a man in a wheelchair appeared from another open doorway.

He opened his mouth to greet the man, then snapped it shut as his brain struggled to process what he was seeing. After a beat, he came out with, "Christ! What in God's name happened to you?"

A strangled sound came from behind him, and the woman hurried to stand between Lucas and the man in the wheelchair, her face the epitome of fury. "What the hell is *wrong* with you? You can't speak to people like that! How rude, how disgusting—I'm calling your boss, right now!" Shooting Lucas a venom-filled glance, she stepped over to a side table holding a landline phone and picked up the receiver.

"Hey, hey," said the man in the wheelchair, manoeuvring himself over and gently taking the woman's wrist. "It's okay. It's okay."

"No, it's damn well not," she fumed, glaring at Lucas once more. "He can't go around speaking to people like that."

"Seriously, it's okay. I *know* him. Now put the bloody phone down."

Lucas watched the exchange in utter confusion and remained silent. What his brain was telling him and what his eyes were telling him were two completely different things.

Once the other man was happy there would be no phone call taking place, he gave the woman a reassuring pat on the arm and wheeled himself over to Lucas. Holding out his hand, he said, "Good to see you again, Lucas. It's been a while."

Still in a daze, Lucas took the offered hand and shook it, but it was several long seconds before he managed to formulate a reply. "You too, Greg. But seriously… what happened?"

Greg looked down at his legs with a wry expression, then back up at Lucas. "Believe it or not, I broke my back in a skiing accident. Fucking ridiculous, huh? We've battled arseholes and terrorists together in the desert and managed to stay in one piece, but put me on a snowy hill with boards strapped to my feet and this is what happens."

Shaking his head, Lucas said, "I'm really sorry, mate. I don't mean to stand here gawping, but I just can't process it. I didn't have a clue."

"Why would you?" His gaze shifted briefly to the woman, then back. "You left the army; we lost touch. I left the army and took a little bit of time out, and this was my reward. Seems I would have been safer dodging IEDs and suicide bombers."

Lucas recognised the sarcastic humour his old friend was employing, but he couldn't bring a smile to his lips—his whirling brain wouldn't allow it. How was it possible that his old comrade, his friend, a fantastic soldier, had been paralysed in the pursuit of leisure? It just didn't compute.

"Mate." Greg waved his hand in front of Lucas's face. "I understand you're in shock, but please could you stop looking at me like that? I get it, really I do, but no amount of feeling sorry for me is going to help. I've had time to get used to it, come to terms with it, and I'm fine. Plus, when have you ever known me to give up? I've been told it's unlikely I'll ever walk again, but not impossible. So I'm clinging to that and clocking some serious time in the gym and with my physio. This is just temporary."

Nodding slowly, Lucas replied, "Yes. Yes, you're right. Okay, great." The smile he conjured wasn't a wide one, but it *was* genuine. "It really is good to see you, buddy." He clapped Greg on the shoulder and turned to the woman. "And I'm really sorry for upsetting you, Mrs. Judd. I was just completely gobsmacked. Are you, um—"

"This is my sister, Violet," Greg interjected. "Violet, this is Lucas Hartley, an old army mate of mine." He continued as the other two nodded acknowledgment at each other. "I'm actually very independent, despite my predicament, but I thought it'd be a good idea to have Violet here while the smoke detectors were fitted. She's much more sensible with this kind of stuff than I am."

"Fair enough." Lucas shrugged. "Now, speaking of fitting smoke detectors, I'd better get on with it before the guys in the truck send out a search party." There was more he wanted to say, lots more, but he wasn't going to breathe a word of it while Violet was in earshot.

"Can I get you a drink?" Violet asked.

Normally Lucas would decline such offers, wanting to get his job done and get out as fast as possible—especially if he was being flirted with—but this situation was different, and not one he'd have imagined, not in a million years. After all this time, he was seeing Greg Barnett again. He was in no rush to get away. Apparently Greg's magnetism hadn't faded over time, or as a result of his new circumstances.

"Uh, yes," he finally said, realising his brain had got carried away and he hadn't actually replied to the question. "That would be great, thanks. Maybe a cup of tea?"

"Plenty of milk, two sugars," added Greg, before Lucas got time to finish.

He remembered how I take my damn tea. Christ.

"That's right, isn't it, Lucas?" Greg grinned at him, a twinkle in his green eyes.

Nodding and turning a smile on Violet, he said, "Yes, that's right. If it's not too much trouble."

"Not at all." Violet turned and headed through the archway Greg had first come out of when Lucas had arrived, which presumably led to the kitchen.

"So," Lucas said, a little too brightly as he began to unpack his equipment, "other than the obvious, what have you been up to since I last saw you? You're not married, I take it?"

After shooting a glance in the direction of the kitchen, Greg turned back to him with a glare. "No," he said quietly, "I'm not married. Why in God's name would I be married?"

The mood in the room had gone from jovial to glacial in the space of a couple of seconds. Feeling petulant, Lucas shrugged. "Oh, I dunno. Because it's what people do, perhaps?"

"Not people like us," Greg ground out, his eyes narrowed.

"Oh!" Pressing a hand theatrically to his heart, Lucas replied, "So you're admitting it now, are you? *People like us,* huh? Well, this is progress indeed."

"What's progress?" Violet asked as she came back into the room, carrying two mugs. She handed one each to Lucas and Greg, then returned for a third one, which she cradled in her hands as she looked at Lucas, still awaiting a response.

"Your brother has finally decided where he wants the detectors. He's just as indecisive as I remember." On the surface, the words were harmless enough, but Lucas knew Greg would understand the subtext, which, of course, was why he'd said it. Now the shock was wearing off, the resentment had started to seep through. It was hardly a surprise, given the number of things they'd left unsaid.

Violet was either completely unaware of the tension between the two men, or was blatantly ignoring it. "Well that's great. Do you want to get started?"

Thirty minutes later the smoke detectors were installed and had been tested, and Lucas had run through some fire safety information with the two of them—made particularly complex by

Greg's situation. He was more than ready to leave. Questions and snide comments were rapidly building up in his brain, and every moment he remained in Greg's presence risked him opening his mouth and blurting them out.

With a huge sense of relief, he grabbed his stuff and said his goodbyes. "I'll see myself out." After striding away before Greg or Violet could stop him, Lucas had the door open and one foot out before Greg's voice halted him in his tracks.

"Uh, don't you need your helmet?"

Lucas spun to see Greg behind him, the offending helmet in his hand. He took it without a word and turned back towards the truck.

"I've gotta know, mate. Why do you bring your helmet into people's houses to fit smoke detectors? It's not that dangerous a job, surely?"

Exhaling a heavy breath, Lucas replied, "Because, *mate,* quite often the houses in question have kids who, when faced with a fireman in uniform, want to see him in the full get-up."

Quirking an eyebrow, Greg shot back, "I can't say I blame them. I've never much been one for a man in uniform—probably because I wore one for so long myself—but you," he made a gesture that encompassed Lucas's fire-retardant outfit, "look damn good dressed like that. Totally hot, if you'll pardon the pun." After glancing behind him to make sure Violet wasn't hovering, he continued, "You can break down my bedroom door any time. Even if my house isn't on fire." He winked.

Lucas glanced over his own shoulder to make sure his

colleagues weren't paying too much attention, then leaned down close to Greg's ear and said, his voice dripping with fury, "This isn't over, smart arse. I'm coming back after my shift and we're having this out. Make sure your sister isn't here."

"Okay," Greg said, too cheerily, "that's fine. Well, I'm not going anywhere, am I?" He indicated his legs and grinned at Lucas.

With a grunt, Lucas spun around again and marched back to the fire truck, trying hard to rein in his temper. The last thing he needed was for his colleagues to notice he was behaving oddly. They'd ask questions, and they'd ask them until they got answers.

Somehow, he managed to wrestle a neutral expression onto his face as he headed along the garden path. Having forced the tension out of his body, he opened the truck door as normally as possible and clambered inside before placing the equipment on the floor and nodding casually to his workmates. "Damn, that was boring. I was almost wishing for a bloody emergency. But it's another one checked off the list. Ready to roll, lads?"

*****

Lucas kept up the cool façade right until the end of his shift. After saying goodbye to his colleagues, he grabbed his car keys and hurried out, still in his uniform. His hasty exit garnered lots of comments along the lines of "Where's the fire?" and "He must be on a promise," but he didn't care. He'd have to explain his actions the following day, but he'd deal with that then. Right now, he needed to get to Greg's place and let spill the words that had been building up in his mind ever since he'd laid eyes on him again. If he didn't get it all off his chest soon, he'd explode.

Driving a little faster than the legal speed limit, but not so much as to be dangerous or draw attention, Lucas relied on memory alone to get him to the house. Fortunately, his memory served him correctly, and he parked up, leapt out of the car and strode up the garden path again. He knocked on the door harder than was necessary, then waited. Greg couldn't exactly run to the door, could he?

The thought depleted his ire a little, but Lucas allowed it to flare back up again. He refused to feel sorry for Greg. For starters, his old friend didn't *want* his sympathy, and also, if anyone was going to overcome a major back injury and walk again, it would be Greg. Stubborn could be his middle name. *Should* be his middle name, actually. That particular personality trait was what had caused the problems between them in the first place.

When Greg eventually opened the door to an irritable, sweaty, slightly grubby Lucas, he simply backed up and indicated Lucas should enter the house. Closing the door, he said, "Go sit down in the living room. I'll be right in."

Lucas headed through to the living room as requested, then settled onto one of the leather chairs and waited for Greg to follow him, ready to open his mouth and let all the bad feelings tumble out.

As Greg wheeled himself into the room, he asked, "Can I get you a drink? Something to eat?"

"I didn't come here for a three-course meal, Greg. I came here to talk. So make sure you're sitting comfortably because I've got plenty to say."

Greg raised his eyebrows and pursed his lips, then nodded slowly. "All right. We're alone, and I'm not expecting anyone. So talk." He folded his arms and waited expectantly.

Taken aback at Greg's apparent willingness to listen, Lucas was temporarily rendered dumb. He quickly realised that it wasn't because he didn't know what to say, more that he had *too much* to say, and didn't know where the hell to start. He thought for a moment, then decided to start with the question that had been burning away inside him since the last time they'd seen each other all those years ago. No doubt the conversation would develop naturally from there.

"Great. So, I'm just gonna come right out with it, Greg. Are you fucking gay, or what?"

A spluttering laugh came from Greg's lips, and his eyes widened. "What? What kind of a question is that?"

Glowering, Lucas replied coolly, "One I'd like the answer to, please. An answer I think I'm *entitled* to. So, do you like men, or were you just leading me on, toying with me?"

The accusations seemed to tip Greg's disbelief and confusion into anger. "No, Lucas, I was not leading you on, *or* toying with you. It just wasn't that bloody simple, was it? It was a long time ago. Being gay in the army wasn't something people would have accepted as easily—"

"I wasn't expecting us to go public, Greg. I *know* what it was like. I was there, remember? And for the record, I don't think it's exactly easy to be gay in the army, even now—though I'm sure attitudes are much improved since our day. But it was more than that, wasn't it? It wasn't just worrying about what people would think, what people would say. You hid behind all that because you were scared of admitting what was between us, scared of letting it happen and seeing what happened next. You used it as a bloody excuse, and yet thought it was okay to be the way you were with me, so intimate… and yet not. So many times we were close to… something, and yet you always backed off in the end. I thought I was going fucking crazy, Greg! Thought I was imagining the whole bloody thing. It's only now, having had all the time since to think about it, figure it out, that I realised you were just being a complete and utter coward. It felt like you didn't really want me, but you didn't want anyone else to have me, either. Not that there ever *was* anyone else, but if I was wrapped up in you, I wouldn't even look elsewhere."

Greg ran his hands through his hair, then slammed them down on the arms of his wheelchair, making a slapping sound reverberate through the room.

He looked *furious,* madder than Lucas had ever seen him. *Good.* Maybe now he'd say what he really thought, instead of bottling it up and hiding behind a multitude of stupid excuses.

"You know what," Greg said, his voice full of venom, "you're right."

"Whaaat?"

"You're right," he repeated, his tone much more neutral now, the anger physically seeping from his posture and changing into something that looked more like defeat. "*Most* of what you just said.

It wasn't deliberate, and I certainly never meant to hurt you, but I wanted you. Really wanted you, but I didn't have the balls to go through with it. I knew once, *if,* we crossed that line then there would be no going back. People would know we were together even if we didn't tell them because I simply wouldn't be able to hide how I felt about you. I *was* scared. Scared of people knowing, commenting, disapproving, thinking it would somehow affect how good we were at our jobs."

Greg ran a hand through his hair again, took a shaky breath. "But mostly I was terrified if I let myself take that final step towards being with you, loving you, that something would happen to you. And there was no way I'd be able to cope with that. So yeah, I didn't want anyone else to have you, but only because I wanted you so damn badly myself. I fucking *loved* you, Lucas, more than anything, and I couldn't bear the thought of losing you. But through my own idiocy, I lost you anyway, and I've regretted it ever since. I'm sorry. For everything."

Several seconds passed while Lucas let Greg's words sink in. They whirled around his brain, changing opinions long formed, answering questions and raising other ones all at the same time. Soon, the silence became too long, and he had to fill it. "Y-you *loved* me?"

The corners of Greg's lips quirked slightly, as though he was amused that was the first thing Lucas could come out with. "Yes, I did. Completely. And honestly… crazy as it probably sounds, I think I still do."

Lucas raised his eyebrows, then propped his elbows on his

knees and leaned his head in his hands, staring intently at the carpet as the enormity of what had just been said hit him. *Greg used to love me? And possibly still does? Fuck.*

Snapping his head back up, Lucas said, "So why the hell has it taken the world's most ridiculous coincidence of me turning up at your house to fit smoke detectors in order to find all this out? Why didn't you get in touch before now? How can you have let so much time pass, time that we could have…" He didn't finish his sentence. There was no point—just because Greg had admitted his feelings, didn't mean they'd end up together. There were too many what-ifs. Billions of the bloody things.

Greg groaned.

"Hey," Lucas was up and across the room and standing in front of Greg's wheelchair in barely a second. "Are you all right? Do you need anything? A glass of water?"

Greg opened his eyes and looked surprised to see him standing there. He smiled and waved Lucas away. "I'm fine." A chuckle. "I'm sorry, it wasn't that kind of groan. It was one of frustration, irritation, desperation. All aimed squarely at myself." He huffed out a breath. "Guess at this stage there's no point in telling you anything but the truth. Look, Lucas, I said I regretted what *didn't* happen between us, and I meant it. But I didn't realise just how much until this," he indicated his chair, "happened. I know it's a cliché, especially given how many times our lives have been in danger over the years—and yours still is—but until I broke my back, I didn't truly appreciate how short life is."

He closed his eyes momentarily, then continued, "But when I

did, I knew I had to do something about it. About *us*. I knew the chances were I was too late, far too late, and that you could be shacked up with the love of your life, living happily ever after. But I had to try anyway."

Lucas frowned. "But you didn't. You didn't try anything. We wouldn't even be having this conversation if it weren't for a bunch of coincidences. Unless you—"

"No, I didn't know. I didn't set this up. You turning up at my house earlier was as much of a shock to me as it was to you. You see, the idea was for me to find you once I was better. Walking again. I didn't want you to see me like this, in this damn chair. You've seen me drive tanks, run carrying wounded men, shooting the shit out of terrorists. I just didn't want you to see me in this state."

He actually looked embarrassed now, colour tingeing his cheeks as he tugged out the non-existent crumples in his jeans. "You were my carrot, if you like. I dangled you, the possibility of seeing you again and trying to put things right, in front of myself. Used it to spur me on, to get me fighting, making progress. And only when this wheelchair was a thing of the past was I going to allow myself a reward. Even if that reward was no longer available. Seeing you, apologising, admitting my feelings was enough. At least then I'd be able to move on with my life."

Lucas rubbed his face, then blinked rapidly. It all made sense, but was still so utterly crazy it made his head hurt. How was it possible that he'd started the day expecting the most dramatic thing to happen would be a house fire?

"Do you want a cup of tea?" Greg asked.

Lucas couldn't help but laugh. The pair of them were so bloody British it was ridiculous. Things get tough—have a cup of tea. "Yes, please."

Greg smiled in response and wheeled himself through the doorway into the kitchen.

Relaxing into the chair, Lucas looked around him. He believed every word Greg had said—after all, he'd never lied to him before, so why would he start now? Particularly, he believed the part about his friend being determined to put the wheelchair behind him. The house was just that—a house, not a bungalow—and although certain things had been arranged to make life easier for Greg, there was nothing too permanent. Nothing that couldn't be removed, erased from memory when the time was right.

In that moment, Lucas decided he wanted to be there for Greg when that time came. No matter what happened between them, or if nothing happened, he wanted their friendship back. He *missed* him, for Christ's sake! They'd been the best of friends, and had it not been for those romantic feelings getting in the way and fucking everything up, he was confident they'd still be the best of friends. Laughing, joking, chatting about everything and nothing… despite the horrific things they'd seen and done in the army, they'd been the happiest days of Lucas's life, and it was all down to Greg. The army he could live without—he loved being a fireman just as much—but Greg? He needed him back in his life, to stay. The fact he was in a wheelchair was utterly irrelevant—the man he loved was just the same.

He was smiling to himself when Greg returned, a tray on his lap holding two mugs of tea. Once he was close enough, he held one out to Lucas, who took it with thanks.

"No, thank *you*."

Lucas frowned. "Why, what did I do?"

"You didn't try to help. Most people try to help, or take over, assuming I can't make a bloody drink by myself."

Shrugging, Lucas replied, "I've made you enough fucking cups of tea over the years. It's about time you returned the favour."

His eyes glinting, Greg lifted his mug in a salute. "Fair enough. Bottoms up."

A silence, companionable this time, fell over them as they sipped their drinks. When he'd finished the sweet beverage, Lucas reached over and placed his empty mug on a coaster on the table beside him.

"So," he said, looking at his friend, "what happens now?"

Greg glanced down at his mug, then back up at Lucas almost shyly. "Well, um, I guess it depends."

"On?"

"You. This, us meeting, talking, has happened way sooner than I'd planned, but it doesn't change the way I feel. But if you're not available…"

"I am," Lucas replied quickly. He saw no sense in stringing it out. They'd wasted enough time. "I'm available, Greg. I always have been. It's the soppiest, girliest cliché ever, so don't you dare breathe a word to anyone else, but it's always been you, for me. I'm not saying I've been the Virgin Mary, but it's only been physical—

nothing more. So, if you want to give it a go, I'm game."

Greg downed the rest of his tea and dumped the mug and tray on the nearest table. "It doesn't bother you that I'm... like this? That I could be like this forever?"

"Like what, Greg? You're still *you*. You just sit on your arse all the time." He winked. "Seriously, though, even if you never walk again, I'll still want you. It doesn't make the slightest bit of difference to me. But I know you. You *will* walk again. I don't know when, but I'll be here when you do. If that's what you want."

Nodding profusely, Greg wheeled himself closer. "Yes. Yes. But... that's not all I want."

Lucas raised his eyebrows in a question. "It isn't?"

"No." A wicked grin spread across Greg's face. "You know how I said you looked hot in that uniform? Well, I meant it. But I'd also rather like to see what you look like stripping out of it. And fucking me. Christ, we've experienced enough sexual tension to last several lifetimes. I think we should give in to it, so we can move on with slightly clearer heads." He tipped Lucas a wink. "I say slightly because, well, we've got a lot of time to make up for. I don't think once is going to be enough. Do you?"

Letting out a laugh that came right from his belly, Lucas shook his head. "No, I don't. But, um, at the risk of sounding insensitive, how is it going to work?"

"Oh, down there?" Greg pointed at his crotch. "Everything works just fine for me. I can even feel my legs. They just don't work all that well at the moment. But I'm sure we can find workarounds for the time being, right?" When Lucas nodded, he continued, "To avoid any further delays, yes, I have lube and condoms. So, if it's not too much trouble, sexy fireman, could you carry me to my bedroom?"

Half-wondering if he was in some kind of incredibly vivid dream, Lucas nodded, then stood up. He lifted Greg out of the wheelchair and made his way upstairs, careful not to whack his left leg on the stairlift that was Greg's usual way of getting to the upper floor of his house.

"Straight ahead at the top of the stairs," Greg said with a grin.

Without replying, Lucas headed for the door in question, opened it and manoeuvred through without hitting either of them on anything. After kicking the door shut behind them, he crossed over to the bed and lowered Greg to the mattress.

"You don't have to be quite so gentle, you know. I'm not saying dropping me out of a second story window is a good idea, but you can toss me onto the bed without doing any damage."

"Quit your sarcasm and get naked," Lucas growled. "You said it yourself, we've got some lost time to make up for."

Greg did as commanded, and did it way faster than Lucas expected. He was gazing at his friend's naked body before he'd really prepared himself. And damn, it looked just as good as he remembered… better, actually, given the erection that stood proudly from its nest of tight curls. He'd never seen *that* before. His mouth actually watered a little as he drank in the sight—the lithe yet muscled form, the long, thick cock, and the wide grin plastered on his face.

"Your turn, hot fireman," Greg said, raking his gaze up and

down Lucas's body. "Though at some point, we've gotta figure out a way for us to screw while you're wearing the uniform. It's fucking sexy. But right now, I want your skin against mine, your mouth on mine, your cock inside me."

Lucas's response was to shrug off his heavy jacket and let it fall to the floor. Then he removed his boots one by one and let them thump onto the carpet. Next came his braces—the thick straps holding up his trousers—which he tugged off his shoulders before undoing his button and fly and shoving his trousers to his ankles. Stepping out of them, he shot a glance at Greg, who was watching him with a predatory expression. He indicated Lucas should continue.

Grinning, Lucas yanked off his socks, his T-shirt—which elicited a pleased murmur from the direction of the bed—and finally, his boxers. This time the murmur was more of a growl, and Lucas watched as Greg used his strong upper body to move himself across the mattress and retrieve a small bottle of lube and a condom from his bedside table.

Waving them around triumphantly, Greg said, "Please, Lucas, don't make me wait any longer. I want you." With his free hand he grasped his cock, pumping it slowly as Lucas approached the bed and clambered onto it.

Lucas took the items from Greg's hand and put them down. Then he shuffled between Greg's legs and leaned in for a kiss. A long overdue, desperately anticipated kiss.

And it was everything he could have hoped for. Almost immediately, Greg opened his mouth and their tongues came together, tentatively at first, then quickly growing in confidence. Brushing together, intertwining, fighting and thrusting. Lucas became aware their cocks were making similar movements to their tongues—eager for each other.

Grinning against Greg's mouth, Lucas put his weight on his elbows and reached up to tangle his fingers in his lover's dark hair. He used the leverage to pull their mouths even harder together, almost bruisingly. And yet, the slight discomfort, the clashing of teeth, only served to heighten his arousal. It was need, pure need, lust, desire, that drove the two of them, and until they quenched it, things were only going to get more frenzied.

Bring on the frenzy, Lucas thought to himself as he sucked and nipped at Greg's lower lip, enjoying the moans the actions brought forth. God, he wanted to fuck that perfect mouth, stick his cock between those lips and thrust until his cum spilled out. But he wouldn't—not yet, anyway. They had time, time to do that and so many other things, things they'd both no doubt fantasised about many times over the years, and would finally make reality.

After pulling away and dragging in a shaky, much-needed breath, Lucas said, "If we carry on much longer, I'm going to come before we've done any more than kiss. And, weirdly sexy as that might be, I really want to be inside you when I come."

Looking a little dazed—lust-drunk, probably—Greg nodded. "Yes," he whispered, cupping Lucas's face and rubbing his hands across the rough stubble. "Fuck me, Lucas, please."

After leaning down for another smouldering, toe-curlingly erotic kiss, Lucas reluctantly tore himself away. He sat back on his haunches and reached for the lube and condom. Carefully, he opened and rolled on the protection, then set about applying the slippery liquid to his cock and Greg's arsehole. By the time he was done, his dick was so hard it hurt, and Greg was writhing, moaning, and pleading.

Eager to answer that plea, Lucas tossed the bottle of lube to one side and got into position. Gripping the base of his shaft, he glanced up at Greg's face for confirmation and was presented with a frantic nod. Smiling, he shuffled closer, pressed his tip against Greg's slick hole and paused for a moment to gather himself. He didn't want to go too crazy and have it all be over in seconds, not when they'd waited so long.

Sucking in a calming breath through his nostrils, he then forged on, pushing against the tight ring of resistance, pushing until he breached it, then continuing to slide slowly deeper, until he was balls-deep inside the love of his life.

For that's what Greg was, he realised. There'd never been anyone else, not really, and now he knew for a fact there never would be.

Looking down at Greg's ecstatic expression, he managed to force his tongue, lips and voicebox to work together and produce some words. "I love you, Greg. So much."

Greg reached up and grasped the back of Lucas's neck, then yanked him down so they were nose to nose. His expression as serious as his tone, he said, "I love you, too. So *fucking* much. Now please, take that carrot of yours and use it to make us both come."

Almost choking on his sudden laughter, Lucas nodded. "All

right. Since you asked so nicely…"

He was glad, really. There was no way he could have held on much longer. Ridiculous, but it felt as though he'd been holding on to this orgasm for years. As he thrust long and hard inside Greg's grasping arse, he figured he probably had. It was different, so different from anything that had gone before. It wasn't just about bodily functions, about fucking, about coming, about scratching an itch. It was deeper, and although he couldn't truly articulate it, he knew it was because he was where he was meant to be. With the man he was supposed to be with.

It wouldn't be easy. But then when had their lives together ever been easy? All that mattered was putting their mistakes behind them and moving on, as a couple. It truly didn't matter to him if Greg never walked again, but he was sure, given time, that the stubborn man he loved would fight his way back onto his feet. Literally.

The thought of Greg being his, exclusively his, for the rest of their lives was too much—it drove him over the edge. "Uhhh, Greg, I'm gonna come…"

Greg slipped his hand between their bodies and took hold of his own cock. "Do it. I won't be far behind you."

After pushing himself up on his hands, both so he could thrust faster and Greg could toss himself off, Lucas put everything he had into the act. Hard and long and deep and furious, he pounded Greg's backside, relishing the perfection of its grip around his shaft. It was so tight, yet so greedy, and he wanted nothing more than to feed it full of his cum.

Seconds later, the choice was taken from him. His body overruled everything else. Tingles shot through every nerve ending, his sac scrunched up against his body, and a line of blissful, white-hot fire raced from his balls and up out of his dick. He let out a growl as he spurted into the condom again and again, his cock twitching and leaping, Greg's beautiful form prone beneath him. "God, I love you!" he yelled, meeting Greg's gaze.

"I love you, too," Greg replied on a gasp as his own climax hit, ripping through him and making his face contort with pleasure. His stomach and chest were soon covered with cum, and they grinned dopily at each other as they rode out their respective orgasms.

Before long, Lucas's shaky arms would hold him up no longer. Carefully, he pulled out of Greg, then moved over to lie beside him. He reached out and tugged Greg into his grasp. Holding him tight, he pressed a kiss to the mop of damp hair and breathed in his scent. *Perfection.* This was perfection.

Lying there, entwined with his lover, Lucas could still scarcely believe it. But it didn't matter what he believed, only what was happening. And it was happening, right here, right now, and nothing would ever be the same again.

Lucas grinned. Who needed non-existent gay single dads to flirt with, anyway? He finally had the man he'd wanted for years—and he existed, all right. He was real, completely gorgeous and, apparently, ready to go all over again. Yes, he thought as he shuffled down the bed to take Greg's growing cock between his lips, the future was bright. Brighter than the damn sun, and twice as fucking hot.

Out in the Cold
Chapter One

After completing his stretches, Kane Wimborne grabbed his keys and left the house, locked the door behind him and pocketed the keys. He jogged down the driveway before pausing at a keypad to punch in the code that would open the gates and allow him off the property.

He'd barely got through the gates when he saw something that made him stop dead. A human-shaped bundle was lying next to the wall on his left. Instinctively, his hand went to his pocket. Yes, he could phone for help if it was needed.

Cautiously, he approached the shape, with many possibilities running through his head. It could be a homeless person or a drunk who had simply been looking for a sheltered place to sleep. It could be someone who was injured. Or he could be about to step onto a crime scene. Conscious of this last point, he called out before getting any closer—he didn't want to inadvertently mar any evidence, should that unfortunate scenario be the case.

"Hey. You all right?" He felt stupid saying the words, because someone lying next to a wall first thing in the morning couldn't be classified as all right, for whatever reason they were there.

As there was no response, he edged a little closer and was about to shout again when a weird sensation overtook him. A sensation he hadn't felt in a very long time—the one that told him another shifter was nearby.

He'd already been on edge, but now he hurriedly looked around him, confident that even in the dull morning light his superior vision would immediately spot anything out of place. There was nothing. He didn't hear or sense anything, either. Except for the fellow shifter who was on the ground in front of him.

Because it was clear the wall-hugger was a shifter, given Kane's senses told him there was no one else around. There rarely was at 5:30 in the morning. Now Kane realised what a good thing this was—he didn't want any witnesses, just in case any random shifting took place. It was entirely possible—it was a natural response to threats, especially if one was injured.

And if he or she wasn't injured, why in the hell were they here?

No longer bothered about contaminating a crime scene—he wouldn't be calling the authorities on another of his kind, whoever they were—Kane crouched down beside the figure and searched for its neck, then its pulse. He found both, which was a relief, and at the same time ascertained that the "it" was in fact a man. The stubble on the neck and jaw gave it away. It was either that or a bearded lady had absconded from the local circus.

After calling out a couple more times, Kane decided the softly, softly approach was clearly not going to work. Checking the two of them were still alone—since what he was about to do could easily stir the guy into changing—he grabbed the man's shoulders and shook him, hard, then slapped his face for good measure.

It took a few seconds, but finally, the man came round. Groaning, he lifted his hand up to his face, where Kane had hit him.

As the guy attempted to sit up, Kane reached out to help him, then gasped.

He should *not* have slapped his face. All he'd done was add additional pain to an already affected area. A badly abused area, in fact. The other shifter looked like he'd taken a serious beating, or fallen from the top of a very tall tree.

"Christ," Kane said, supporting the man's back, so he didn't flop back down onto the pavement. "What the hell happened to you?"

The man's eyes had opened by now, and his facial expression was a mixture of confusion, pain, and grogginess. Or at least that's how it looked to Kane. Underneath the swelling and bruising, he could have been smiling, for all he knew. Kane helped him to his feet.

"I, uh… can we talk about this somewhere else?" The man looked around, seemingly worried they weren't alone.

"Yes, I suppose. You're right outside my house. We can go in, if you like, get you cleaned up and into some fresh clothes."

Peering down at himself, the man let out a bark of laughter, which sparked a series of hacking coughs. When his lungs finally settled, he groaned again. "Sorry. God, I'm a fucking mess, aren't I? I'm Paul, by the way. Paul Barter. I'd shake your hand, but I don't want you to let go of me in case I fall on my arse again."

"Kane Wimborne. I'd say I'm pleased to meet you, but I'm not sure if I am yet."

"It's really good of you to help me. I could be anyone."

Kane helped Paul towards the gates. "You *are* anyone. But

you're one of my kind. And, given the state you're in, I don't think you could do me any harm, even if you wanted to." He pressed the relevant buttons on the keypad, and the two men made their way slowly through the gates and up the driveway.

"One of your…" Paul tailed off, then winced, clutching his side with his free hand. His other rested across Kane's shoulders. "Wow. I had no idea. I must be hurt worse than I thought—my senses didn't even pick that up. I take it you're not with the other shifters in town. Actually, don't answer that. If you were, you wouldn't be helping me right now. Unless you're taking me inside so no one can see you finish me off."

Kane stopped with just a couple of feet to go before they reached his front door, his heart rate picking up. "What are you talking about, the other shifters in town? And me finishing you off? Did you hit your head?"

"Yes, I hit my head, but that's not why I'm saying it. Look, can we just sit down somewhere and I'll tell you everything. If you don't want me in your house, that's fine. We can sit on the step."

"Don't be stupid. We need to get you in the warm."

Paul's bruised and swollen face twisted into a smile, though it looked more like a grimace. "Yes, boss." They started moving again.

A feeling of unease swept through Kane, but he said nothing, simply retrieving his keys and letting them into the house. After kicking the door shut behind them, he half-carried Paul over to the sofa and plopped him down. "I'm going to go and get you a glass of water, and then you can tell me what the hell happened."

Paul merely nodded.

In the kitchen, Kane grabbed a glass and filled it with water, popped a couple of painkillers out of a packet in the drawer, then went back into the living room. Paul hadn't moved, and despite the fact he was now in out of the cold, he looked worse than he had when Kane had first seen him.

He handed Paul the glass and tablets, then claimed the chair opposite.

Paul quickly downed the pills, along with half the contents of the glass.

"Ready to talk?" His words came out harsher than he'd intended, especially since there was no denying that Paul was in a bad way, even with his accelerated healing powers. But things had been quiet for so long that the fact shifters were back in town did not make him happy.

Paul gulped down the remainder of the liquid, swallowed heavily, then began to speak. "I'm here on business. Regular, everyday business. Nothing to do with being a shifter. Last night I went into a bar in town as I was bored sitting alone in my hotel room. I just wanted to be around people for a little while. I had a call of nature and headed for the Gents. There was a group of folk blocking my way, and as I got closer I realised they were shifters, too. Werewolves, to be exact. Figuring they might not notice one more presence, I acted normal and asked one of the women if she would please excuse me so I could get to the bathroom. I was nice as pie, didn't touch her or anything. But it didn't matter." He took a breath, placed the glass down on the end table and wrung his hands together.

"It seems the woman I spoke to was the packmaster's bitch—literally—and he took offence to me speaking to her. Apparently, he's fucking crazy! I explained that I'd just asked her if I could get past, but he wouldn't listen. He ordered me outside to sort things out between us, and seconds later I've got a pack of weres—albeit in human form—beating the crap out of me."

"What a bunch of arseholes."

"That's putting it mildly. As soon as I could get away, I ran. Not exactly brave, I know, but I had no chance against the whole pack. They'd have killed me. I didn't really know where I was going. I just ran and ran. Then I saw some really high walls and thought if I could just get over them, I might have a shot at getting away. But I didn't get a chance. As soon as I got close to the wall they started to slow down, then turned and slunk off, one by one. It was bizarre. I think I just stood there watching them, gobsmacked. The adrenaline must have worn off and I passed out, because the next thing I remember is you waking me up."

Kane raised an eyebrow. Well, that was new. Werewolves running away from walls. This guy must have hit his head really hard. "They just saw the wall and stopped chasing you? Like they were frightened of the wall?"

"Yeah. I know it sounds crazy. Totally fucking barmy. But that's what happened."

"Hmm." He thought for a moment, and came up with nothing. "So, Paul, since my wall frightened off your attackers and I've brought you inside to help you, may I ask, what kind of shifter are you? And why in God's name didn't you shift to get away? You'd have been faster. Unless you change into a tortoise. Or a snail."

Paul smirked, apparently feeling a little better. The painkillers and his speedy healing must have been kicking in. "No, I don't change into a tortoise. Not usually, anyway. I, um, I can change into anything. Anything I can visualise."

Chapter Two

This time, both of Kane's eyebrows went up, and they almost disappeared into his hairline. "Oh. Okay. So I repeat my other question: why the hell didn't you change to get away? You could have become a bird. I know shifters that can change into anything at all are rare, but surely it was worth risking exposing that fact to get away?"

"Lots of reasons. One, someone other than the weres might have seen me. Two, I'm not one hundred per cent sure they even realised I was a shifter. I think they may have just been looking for someone to pick on. Three, by the time they'd beaten the crap out of me, I didn't really have the energy to shift. Four, if I shifted, wherever I ended up, I'd have ended up there naked. I was just considering it as a last resort when they started taking off, anyway. Which leads me to my question. Why the hell are they frightened of you?"

"Frightened of *me?* I thought you said they saw the walls and got spooked."

Paul crossed his arms and fixed Kane with a *look.* "I did, but you know damn well that something else is going on here. *Nobody* is scared of brick walls, least of all a pack of tough-nut weres. They got frightened when they realised where they were, whose property they were near to. It was almost like there was a forcefield around the place to keep people away—with the exception of me, obviously. So I can only assume those guys know who you are and, for some reason, fear you." He paused, seemingly sizing up Kane for the first time. "You don't look so fearsome to me."

Kane frowned. None of this made any sense. He sighed. "Why don't you go and get cleaned up? Come on, I'll show you where everything is, and get you some new clothes. I'm a little bigger than you, but I guess too big is better than too small."

"Great, thanks."

Kane got up and left the room, Paul close behind him. The man's close proximity made him a little uncomfortable, but he couldn't put a finger on why. He wasn't frightened of him, didn't get a threatening vibe at all. Paul just came across as a guy who had had a shitty night and needed some help. Shrugging off the feeling, Kane instead pondered why the pack that had been on Paul's tail were frightened of him. He didn't even know them.

Upstairs, he opened his bedroom door and went inside. "Okay, let me get you some clothes. The shower's just through there, in the en suite. Unless you'd prefer a bath? I have one in the main bathroom."

When Paul didn't reply, Kane turned from where he was rooting through his drawers for a T-shirt and some tracksuit bottoms or a pair of jeans. The other man was still in the hallway, gazing around him, open-mouthed.

"Hey, Paul. What are you doing?"

Snapped out of it, Paul quickly stepped into the room, a sheepish grin on his face. "Sorry, mate. I just got a bit distracted by the house. It's a fucking amazing place, I have to say. Huge. What do you do for a living? Because I'm thinking a change of career is in order."

Kane rolled his eyes. Too many people in the past had been

so impressed with his house, his wealth, that they'd barely even noticed the man behind them. "Yeah, thanks. So, do you want a bath or a shower?"

His tone of voice clearly got through to Paul, as the other man's sheepish grin remained in place, widened even. "A shower would be great, thanks."

After handing him the bundle of clothes he'd put together, Kane led Paul into the bathroom. "Okay, there's toiletries and stuff here. Towels are in that cupboard. Knock yourself out. I'll sort out something to eat while you're in here. But don't rush."

With a tight smile, he left the room, closed the door behind him and headed back downstairs. He wasn't really angry at Paul as such, more frustrated. He reminded himself that if the roles were reversed, he'd be impressed with the house, too. It *was* very beautiful, which, of course, was one of the reasons he'd bought it. Another being the epic security measures, which he'd then added to and enhanced. He had a lot of enemies, so if they found him, he wanted to make sure they couldn't get to him. Not without him being tipped off first, anyway.

As he cut some bread and warmed up some soup, he wondered if it was a coincidence that Paul had found this house, found him. He'd been absolutely right when he said the type of shifter that could change into anything was very rare. So rare that the fact two of them were now in the same house was impossible. Though obviously it wasn't impossible, because it was happening.

Kane had to resist the temptation to go and grab one of his expensive bottles of whiskey. Paul's presence was bringing lots of stuff back to him that he'd buried long ago. Memories of his parents, his brothers, the rest of the pack. How he'd gone from being a lone shifter hiding in the cellar of the ruined house to still being a lone shifter, but one with money, influence, and people who feared him.

He was just pouring the heated soup into two bowls when Paul reappeared. "Hey, that smells good."

Kane turned. "Good. I take it that means you like soup. It was all I had that I could do quite quickly." He was glad he'd got the words out before he really took in Paul's appearance. He'd healed even more since going upstairs, it seemed, and getting cleaned up, washing the blood off, made him look even better. But what was even more striking was the fact he had no shirt on—he had Kane's T-shirt in one hand, ready to be put on, and his upper body was revealed in all its glory.

And glory it was. In his previously beaten up, shabby state, Paul had looked like a guy with an average physique. But that wasn't the case. Paul was *built,* possibly more so than himself.

Swallowing to try to coax some saliva into his dry mouth, Kane picked up the bowls, carried them over to the breakfast bar and put them down opposite each other. "Sit," he said, gesturing to the bar. "I'll just get some spoons and the bread."

After returning with said items, he took his place on the other side of the bar to Paul, noting, with immense relief, that he'd now put the shirt on. However, that proved Kane's previous assessment that Paul was smaller than he was, was utterly wrong. The material stretched tightly over the bulging arms and torso of his visitor.

"Sorry, mate. I'll find you a bigger one when we've eaten."

"Huh?" He followed Kane's gaze, then shrugged. "Don't worry about it. It's clean, and I'm grateful." With a grin, he picked up a chunk of bread and his spoon and proceeded to eat with gusto.

Kane had to make more of an effort to eat his. Partially because in his mind it was breakfast time, not lunchtime—but he'd wanted to get some warm food into the other man—and partially because his body was now reacting to Paul in a way he'd almost forgotten existed. He was just glad the breakfast bar was hiding his semi-erection.

After a few minutes of contented munching and the clinking of spoons against bowls, the two of them finished their meal at about the same time. Making a happy sound, Paul put his hands on his stomach and grinned. "That's better. Thanks so much. You have been brilliant. Right, I'm sure you're a busy man, so I'm not going to impose on you any longer. If I could just bother you for a carrier bag for my old clothes, I'll be on my way. And once I get these laundered, I'll send them back to you." He pointed to his current outfit.

"Um, okay. I'll get you a bag, but you don't need to worry about the clothes. I have plenty." Kane grimaced when he realised how flippant his words sounded. "I mean, I won't miss them. It's okay. Keep them."

He hopped from the stool, grabbed a carrier from a drawer and handed it to Paul, who'd also got down from the breakfast bar.

"Thanks." Paul moved out to the hallway, then came back with the bag containing his dirty, bloodstained clothes. "Seriously. I really appreciate what you've done. And if you ever feel like sharing what you did to scare the shit out of those guys, just let me know. I think it might come in handy—in case I bump into them again."

"You're not leaving town?"

Paul frowned. "Uh, no. I'm supposed to be here for a few more days. I've gotta work." He waved a hand. "I'll be fine. I'll just stay out of everyone's way, and definitely not go back to that bar. They'll probably assume I did a runner, so hopefully they won't be looking for me."

"A-are you sure? I don't want to find you all battered and bloodstained again."

Smiling, Paul replied, "I'm a big boy. I can look after myself." He strode into the hallway, Kane close behind.

Resolutely ignoring the double entendre in the first part of the other man's sentence, Kane moved between him and the door. "Wait. Seriously, wait. Do you have to be at work just yet? It's only," he glanced at his watch, "6:45. You wanna come sit down a minute, discuss this? Perhaps I can help."

Paul looked unsure for a minute, then he placed the bag down next to the hat and coat rack. "No, I don't have to be at work just yet. Okay, let's talk. But I'm warning you, since you started this, I have more than a few questions of my own."

As Kane led the other man back towards the living room, he couldn't help wondering if he'd regret his decision to dissuade him from leaving just yet.

Chapter Three

Kane was just about to sit down when he remembered his manners. "Take a seat. Can I get you another drink?"

"Stop delaying the inevitable, Kane. You wanted to discuss, so let's discuss."

Kane held his hands up and flopped down onto the nearest seat. "All right, all right. So, as I say, I think I can probably help you with the wolf problem. Well, I can make sure they don't go near you again, anyway."

Paul raised an eyebrow. "And how do you propose to do that? Hire me a bodyguard?"

"Of sorts." He paused. "Listen. Can I trust you?"

"Trust me? Of course. I can keep my mouth shut. And even if I couldn't, I got no one to tell anyway."

Kane took that as a valuable piece of information about Paul's life. It sounded as though he, too, had no friends or family to speak of. Another thing they had in common. "Okay. Well, uh, I think I figured out why the wolves wouldn't come near my property."

"You did?"

"Yes. I think… it's because they know who I am."

"Know who you are? What's that supposed to mean?"

"If you'll stop interrupting me, I'll tell you."

"Sorry." Paul looked suitably chagrined.

"You see, you and I have a lot in common. We're, uh, both a certain type of shifter." He carried on speaking, even as Paul's mouth dropped open. "And we're both loners, because of that fact.

My family was killed years ago, when I was a child. I escaped only by chance. They were murdered by a local werewolf pack that discovered what we were. For a long time, we'd fitted in with them, pretending to be regular werewolves, like them. Changing at every full moon, and so on. We had no trouble from them. But somehow, they found out the truth. And it scared them. I think you can figure out the rest."

The empathy in Paul's eyes was clear. "Yes, I think I can. And I'm sorry about your family. Please, carry on."

After pulling in a deep breath, Kane continued. "Thank you. Well, for some time afterwards, I struggled. I was only a child, after all. Just ten years old. I knew the most important thing, after survival, was to keep what I was a secret. Fortunately, as you know, we're not governed by the moon, not forced to shift, so for all intents and purposes, I could appear completely human, one hundred percent of the time. Then I got lucky. A family took me in, and until I was sixteen, things were great. They'd lost a child of their own, so when they found me rummaging in their bins, they were horrified and wanted to help me. I didn't tell them the whole truth, naturally, just that my family had been killed and I was all alone. Perhaps it was just that I was in the right place at the right time, but they didn't question me any further, and we quickly became a family. It was wonderful."

Biting his lip, Kane fell silent for a moment in an attempt to get a handle on his emotions. "*They* were wonderful. But," he couldn't prevent anger seeping into his tone, "somehow, part of the same pack that destroyed my real family found me, and they made a second attempt on my life. Once again, they didn't succeed, but they murdered my foster parents. I was devastated. They were innocent people, even more innocent than my parents and siblings. They were *human,* for heaven's sake! I took off, and started training. I poured my grief, my rage, my disgust, into working out. And, when I was ready, I went out, found those bastards, and got my own back."

"Wow." Paul's eyes were as round as saucers.

"Yeah. I just flipped. Decided there was no way I was going to spend the rest of my life on the run, having those fuckers kill anyone I cared about, anyone I knew. So I went out, and I killed them first. I tracked them down, one by one, and got my revenge. As you can imagine, I gained somewhat of a reputation amongst the were community. But once I was done, I stopped. I killed only those who were involved—not their friends and family. There had been enough violence, and I had no intention of stooping to their level. By that point, however, anyone who had heard of me was terrified of me. I moved up to the wilds of Scotland for a while until everyone forgot about me. Then I came back here and have tried to live a quiet life ever since. But, apparently, someone knows who I am, what I did. And it seems my reputation is intact. I'm more fearsome than you thought, eh?" He sighed, ran a hand through his hair. "Ugh, I hope this doesn't mean I have to move again. I like it here."

Paul shook his head. "I don't think so. It was pure fear I saw in those werewolves. And that was just on seeing your property. They didn't even see *you.* I don't think you have anything to worry about. So, um, I'm not sure what else to say. I get it. I totally get it, what you did. I would have done the same. But my family died in a car crash. I was overseas at the time. They weren't murdered. So I'm just me. A loner by choice, because I don't want to get close to someone and have to keep such a big secret from them."

Kane nodded. He could see the logic in that. "I'm sorry about your family. So, why are you here? In the area, I mean. What do you do for work?"

"Oh." Paul let out a sharp laugh. "Nothing exciting. I'm a rep for a soft drinks company. I'm visiting local independent stores, trying to get them to stock our stuff. It's dull as fuck, but it works for me. Nobody takes too much notice of me. I move around a lot, don't get too friendly with folk. What about you? I'm gonna hazard a guess it's something a bit more interesting than my job. Not to mention lucrative."

"I'm in import-export. But I don't really get involved anymore. I just oversee it. I've got a great team behind me."

"Cool. Good for you. So, what do you do with your days, if you don't mind me asking? Besides running?"

"Running?" He'd almost forgotten he was wearing his running gear. He glanced down at his outfit and laughed. "Yeah, I run. I hike, I climb. And I…" He trailed off.

"Aww, come on, you what? You can't leave me hanging like that."

"Come on, I'll show you."

Kane got to his feet and made for the garden. Paul followed. The sky was growing much lighter now, so the two of them didn't have to rely on their enhanced vision to see what was out there. Kane turned to Paul, watching the other man's reaction to what he was showing him. The stunned yet impressed expression told him everything he needed to know, but he couldn't help asking, just to be sure. "You like?"

Paul snapped his mouth closed, then grinned. "This is *incredible.* You did all this?"

"Everything from digging out the pond to watering the plants. I enjoy it."

"You're a man with as many talents as you have secrets."

Kane shrugged. "You know my biggest secrets now. And that's more than I've told anyone… well, ever."

"Seriously? Well, I appreciate it. But I can't help wondering why. Surely not just because I'm like you?"

"Do you know what, I don't actually have any idea. Our, um, *similarities* are probably part of the reason." He pondered Paul's question further as they admired the garden, until a realisation hit him square between the eyes, causing him to step back.

"Fuuuck." The pull he felt towards the other man grew stronger. It was going to be trouble, he just knew it.

"Hey, are you all right?" Paul's concerned tone cut through the thoughts whirling through Kane's mind.

"Yeah, I'm fine." His tone sounded abrupt even to his own ears, and he had to bite back an apology. The last thing he wanted to do was give the guy the wrong idea. "Anyway, we kinda went off on a tangent there, didn't we? Oversharing and all that." He let out a bark of laughter. "So, as I said before, I can help keep those wolves away from you. Or at the very least, stop them hurting you, should you cross paths."

"Uh, okay. That would be great. So what's the plan?"

"Oh, it's simple really. I put you under my protection."

Paul squinted thoughtfully. "In a human sense, or a paranormal one?"

Ah, the man was smarter than he'd given him credit for. "A paranormal one. It's simple, but effective."

"What does it involve?"

"We both have to shift into the same form, and then I bite you." Even as he said the words, he felt his cock swell, and every *other* inch of him screamed that this was a bad idea. A very bad idea. Although doing this was undoubtedly going to benefit Paul, it would do quite the opposite for him. It would awaken yearnings he'd long forgotten—in both man and beast—and he wasn't sure how he'd be able to get rid of those yearnings once they'd arisen. The idea of shifting back to human form then scurrying to the bathroom to toss himself off was so undignified. Pathetic, really.

"Right. So how exactly does this work? How does you biting me protect me? Sorry, but I don't know anything about this stuff."

You and me both, buddy. Kane had never done anything like it before. All his knowledge was purely theory—he'd never had the chance for practical application before. He didn't even know if it would work. But given the doubt and, if he wasn't mistaken, fear on the other man's face, he was going to act confident, like he knew what he was doing. He'd been figuring things out as he went along for years, and he was doing okay.

"It's, um, a pack thing. Like an alpha thing. If I bite you, I'm claiming you as part of my pack, which immediately brings you under my protection. Any fear those arseholes have of me will automatically apply to you, too. I know it's a little weird, especially since we barely know each other, but it's a means to an end. Once it's done, you can go ahead and live your life however you want. I'll be your alpha in name only—I won't make you do anything. You won't have to live here. You won't even have to see me ever again, if you don't want to."

"So we'll essentially both still be lone… whatever we are. Lone shifters."

"Yes."

"But I'll be under your protection."

"Yes."

"And all we have to do is shift into the same form, and you bite me?"

"Yes."

"Well, when you put it like that, how can I refuse? It sounds so simple."

Chapter Four

Oh, if only it were simple. Kane forced a smile onto his face and nodded. "Just a bite, and you'll be protected. Like a vaccine, only the protection is instant."

"Okay. Do you want to do this now? Will it take long? I don't mean to rush you, only I do have to be at work in a little bit. It may be a shitty job, but it's the only one I've got."

"No problem. You can be on your way pretty quick. It depends how long it takes you to shift."

Paul shrugged. "Not long. What are we gonna shift into, then?"

Kane thought for a moment, then flashed the other man a grin. "Wolves, of course. It'll be a kind of poetic justice, don't you think? That we can become wolves whenever we want to, not when the moon dictates. And we'll be better wolves than those guys, too. They deserve to fucking fear us. We could change into elephants and stomp on them, if we wanted to."

Paul mirrored his grin. "I like your thinking. Okay, let's go for it."

Immediately, both men began stripping. Kane deliberately left his jogging bottoms and boxers until last because his cock was still semi-hard, and the view he was about to get of Paul's body, coupled with what they were about to do, would easily give him a full-on erection. As soon as he was down to his bottoms and underwear, he grabbed both their waistbands and lowered them, bending at the same time to cover his excitable crotch area. Then, without straightening up again, he shifted. It took a good few seconds, because he hadn't transformed for some time. He heard and felt the crack and pop of his bones, sinews and muscles, the stretch and tingle of his skin as it altered and grew fur, the lengthening and sharpening of his finger and toenails into claws.

And then it was over.

When he looked up, another wolf stared back at him. A wolf the same height as his, but more heavyset. It seemed their wolf forms mirrored their human forms, to an extent. Kane saw no reason to hang around any longer. The other man—or creature, as he was now—had agreed to this, so they may as well get on with it. The sooner he did it, the sooner Paul would walk out of his door, out of his life, allowing Kane to get back to normal. He'd try to forget he'd ever met another shifter like him, try to forget how attracted he'd been to him. How he could have made a proper pack. Or a partnership, anyway.

Mentally, he shook his head. No, he was doing the right thing here. It couldn't be like that—Paul didn't even swing that way. There was no point lusting over a straight guy. It was torture, pure and simple. A bite, a goodbye, and it would all be over.

He moved forward, growing used to the loping stride of his wolf. Because it had been a while since he'd shifted into anything, never mind a wolf, it felt odd. But somehow so right. When he was next to Paul, he nudged him, his arousal growing as his head lolled to the side, exposing his furry neck. Without hesitation, Kane opened his jaws, then clamped them around the side of Paul's neck, careful not to sink too deep. His intention was to puncture skin and maybe a little muscle—not to touch any blood vessels or major arteries. This was claiming, not killing.

Perhaps it was difficult because he'd only ever done the latter. And then only when a person or creature deserved it. Now, he was inflicting pain for an utterly different reason. A reason he suspected was going to cause him a great deal of anguish. For as Paul's blood trickled into his mouth, then coated his tongue and seeped down his throat, he knew exactly what was going on. What he'd suspected earlier was coming to fruition.

His animal side, the feral side of him he so rarely let out to play anymore, wanted Paul to be his mate. And not just in the sexual sense. In the soulmate, part of a pack, spending-our-lives-together sense. *Fuck.* Why? Was it desperation? He hadn't got laid in a while, and the number of relationships—meaningful or otherwise—he'd had in his lifetime amounted to a big fat zero. So now the first shifter that comes along in years happens to be the same sort of shifter as him, and his animal side goes and wants him, bad. So bad it hurt.

Realising he still had his jaws clamped around Paul's throat, Kane quickly pulled away. The claiming had worked—there was no reason to keep his teeth sunk into the other wolf's flesh. Now he needed to change back and get the other man out of his house as soon as possible, before things got any more complicated.

As he approached the pile of clothes he'd discarded, Kane began the transformation back to human form, all the sensations he'd experienced earlier running through him in reverse. His claws had barely finished receding when he yanked his boxer shorts and joggers back on. He needed to cover his dick, and fast, because it was now the hardest it had ever been, and was flat-out refusing to behave. It throbbed and twitched; his balls heavy, achy, and eager to be emptied.

For Christ's sake. He'd just done a good deed for someone, and this was how he was repaid? Being laden with the mother of all crushes on a straight guy?

He slipped into his T-shirt, but left his socks and trainers, figuring as soon as he got Paul out of the house, he'd get changed and head into the office. Anything to take his mind off the other man and what they'd just done. And what he wanted to do.

With a groan, a naked Paul appeared before him, having shifted from his wolf form. A livid red mark on the side of his neck was clearly visible, but the wounds had already closed over. The redness, and therefore any evidence of the bite, would probably be gone within five minutes. The perks of being a shifter.

Against his better judgment, Kane allowed his gaze to move from Paul's neck and rake over the rest of his body. The strong, handsome face. The broad shoulders, muscular arms, beautifully defined chest and stomach, the enticing trail of hair that led down to his…

Kane hurriedly closed his eyes. He could absolutely *not* look at Paul's cock. Not only was it pervy and inappropriate, but it would torture him. Hell, who was he kidding? This was already torture.

"—all right?"

Snapping his eyes open again, Kane asked, "Sorry, what did you say?"

"I asked if you were all right. You looked a little weird just then."

Fortunately, the other man had now pulled on the jeans he'd lent him, and was about to put on the T-shirt. He couldn't get covered up soon enough, in Kane's opinion. The bloody man was driving him to distraction. "No, no, I'm fine. It's just been a while since I shifted. I must be out of practice." He laughed, the sound a great deal more cheerful than he felt.

"Oh right, okay. Well, um, thanks, I suppose. I don't know what else to say. It's been a weird day. I'll get out of your hair now, if there's nothing else that needs to be done."

"Nope, we're done. And you're welcome." The smile he gave Paul was genuine. Despite the raging lust he was struggling to ignore, he didn't regret what he'd done. Paul deserved to be safe, deserved to live his life unmolested, and he was glad he'd helped make that happen. If those wolves ever went near him again, they wouldn't know what hit them. His grin grew wider, until he saw Paul's expression falter. It was then he realised his face—or his lips and teeth at the very least—must be covered in blood. Paul's blood. No wonder he looked a little freaked out.

"Shit, sorry." He dashed into the kitchen, turned on the cold tap and began to rinse off, scooping water between his lips to wash any blood from inside, too. The water ran pink at first, then soon turned clear. Only then did he stop. With a sigh, he splashed his whole face with water, then straightened and shut off the tap.

When he turned, Paul stood there, looking awkward. "Hey," he said softly, "I'm gonna go. Duty calls and all that crap. But I just wanted to say thanks again. I really appreciate what you did. And I'm sorry to have disrupted your day." His hand went up to the spot on his neck. Whether the movement was conscious or not, Kane didn't know. But what he did know was that he didn't want the other man to leave. Ever.

Gritting his teeth, he tried hard to stomp down on the thought. It was stupid, pointless. He was in severe danger of making a fool of himself. "Okay, no worries. I'll see you out."

He fell into step behind Paul and the two of them made their way towards the front door once again. As the other man's back was turned, Kane allowed the full range of his emotions to play out on his face, in the hope that letting them out meant he'd be able to rein them in as they said goodbye. Then he'd go and get changed and head straight for the office. Get on with his life, forget this had ever happened.

He knew repeating the thoughts, emphasising them, wouldn't help them come true, but he had to try anyway. When Paul picked up the bag of his soiled clothes and turned to him, the feelings of arousal that had been coursing through Kane turned to pure need and a sick feeling in his stomach.

For Christ's sake, man, get a grip! You're behaving like a lovestruck teenager.

"Right," Paul said, reaching for the door handle, "I'll get going. Thanks so much for what you did. Really." He shrugged. "I don't know what else to say. Ugh, I already said that."

"Don't go!" Kane gasped as his brain processed what he'd said. He'd *meant* to say "you're welcome" and "goodbye," and instead he'd come out with that. Resisting the temptation to bang his head against the wall, he clapped his hand over his mouth, although it was akin to shutting the stable door after the horse had bolted.

Chapter Five

"What?" A cute frown line appeared between Paul's eyebrows. "What's the matter?"

Kane removed his hand from his mouth. "N-nothing. It's just… oh fuck."

"You're not making any sense."

"Trust me, I know. I think what I'm trying to say is that I don't want you to go. Ever."

Paul's frown line grew deeper, but at the same time, Kane saw a glimpse of something in the other man's eyes. Hope, perhaps? "What are you talking about?" He paused, and a look of realisation crossed his face. "Is this some kind of shifter thing? Something we didn't anticipate?" His lips twitched at the corners, almost a smile.

Kane nodded. *Might as well get it out there.* "Something like that. I really can't explain it. All I know is that since I bit you—before then, actually—I wanted you, bad. Seriously bad. The bite just seemed to… amplify everything. I know I said you could walk out of my life and you'd never have to see me again, but although my mouth let those words come out, every other fibre of my being disagreed. I can't call it love, because we only just met, but my animal side is drawn to yours, and I'm drawn to you. Fuck's sake, are you even gay?"

A bark of laughter tumbled from Paul's lips, and his eyes crinkled at the corners. "Christ, what's going on here? Has that bite bound us together, or something? Didn't you know that would happen?" His sudden mirth seemed to stem from surprise more than anything.

Kane shook his head. "I've never done it before. I told you that."

"Oh. Shit. Well, um, in answer to your question, yes, I'm gay. Right now, that's the only thing I know for sure. This is all so fucking weird. I've got all these feelings and I have no idea where they came from, or how to explain them."

"Tell me about it. But I'm glad you're gay."

"You are?"

"Yeah. Because it means I'm not barking up totally the wrong tree. Come here."

"W-what?"

Suddenly, Kane's animal side was more in control than it had ever been before when he was in human form. He growled. "I said, come here." He held out his hand.

Looking utterly shell-shocked, Paul hurriedly dropped the bag of clothes, stepped forward and put his hand in Kane's. Then he gasped as the other man yanked him closer, clamped his other hand around the back of his neck and pulled him in for a kiss. There was very little humanity there—it was brutal.

Kane's grip around Paul's neck increased. Their mouths crushed together bruisingly. Teeth clashed, tongues quested, thrust. Kane dropped Paul's hand, scooped his arm around the other man's back and pulled him so their entire bodies were flush together. The feeling of Paul's stiff cock through his clothes added another layer of frisson to the encounter, one that ramped up Kane's arousal tenfold, something he hadn't even known was possible. He genuinely felt like he was going to come, right away. It was insanity. This man he'd just met, hardly knew. After helping him, he'd felt an urge to fuck him, then to protect him. Now he was doing both, and it felt better than anything he'd ever experienced before in his life, even better than getting revenge on the wolf pack that had slaughtered his family.

That had to mean something. He couldn't allow himself to believe this was love at first sight—it just wasn't something he thought was possible. But he did now believe that the animal part of shifters could connect on a deeper level, and this was clearly what was happening. It was the only explanation for the overwhelming need he felt for Paul. And it wasn't just about sex, either. He genuinely didn't want Paul to leave his side, ever again. He wanted to be his lover, his partner, his alpha.

He was sure two shifters didn't count as being a pack, but he didn't care. He had no desire for anyone else, in any way, shape, or form. It was mind-blowing, but, figuring it was beyond his control, Kane decided to switch off his brain and just go with the flow of what was taking place right now. And what was taking place felt *good.*

Paul had loosened up, seemingly got over the shock of the weird day so far, and was also going with the flow, his enthusiasm growing every second. He'd wrapped his muscular arms around Kane's neck, and the two of them were now kissing with a ferocity that spoke volumes. Their need for each other was extreme, and their lust needed to be sated—soon. What came after that, well, they'd deal with that then.

For now, Kane wanted to get Paul naked again and this time

get inside him and ride him until their teeth rattled and their balls exploded. His cock throbbed at the thought, and he yanked away from the kiss, only to mutter, "Upstairs, now."

It seemed Paul had readily understood and accepted the submissive role he would play—both sexually and also when their animal sides came out to play. With a nod, he turned and jogged up the stairs. Kane followed close behind, slamming the door once they were both in the bedroom. He grabbed Paul's shoulders and gave him a hard shove onto the bed. Paul ended up sprawled across the duvet on his front, and Kane quickly covered him with his body. He began rocking his shaft against the crease between Paul's arse cheeks and pressing kisses to the back of his neck and behind his ears. Then he nipped the other man's earlobe, chuckling as Paul emitted a groan and bucked his hips.

"Are you ready for me?"

Paul nodded.

"Good, because I really need to fuck you. I need to come inside you so bad it hurts. So this first time is probably going to be a bit fast and furious. But I promise you, after that, we'll take our time. We've got all day."

"W-what about my job?" Paul's voice was muffled by the duvet, but Kane still understood him perfectly.

"Screw your job. You're with me now. You don't need a job. But if you really want one, you need to find one that means you come home to me every night. Either that, or you can just work for me. I'll pay you a decent wage. Now, let's stop talking, eh?"

"Okay."

Kane rolled off Paul and got to his feet, then quickly pulled off his clothes again and discarded them on the floor. A glance across the room assured him that Paul was doing the same. He waited, watched, as the other man's delectable body was revealed once more. Broad shoulders, muscles to die for, a torso so lickable it should have been illegal. This time he didn't try to hide that he was watching, or resist the lure. He simply stared, transfixed, at Paul, his own cock lurching as he saw just how engorged Paul's was. Their need for each other was completely and utterly mutual and apparent, and it was time to give in to it.

"Back on the bed," Kane ordered, crossing to his bedside table and retrieving some lube. A condom was unnecessary—shifters couldn't contract human diseases—but the lube was definitely needed. He was going to be more than a little hard on Paul, and he didn't want to hurt him. Not badly, anyway. He was sure the other man could take a spot of discomfort.

He hopped onto the mattress, tossed the bottle down beside him, then reached for Paul. They were drawn together like magnets, and Kane slipped his hand behind Paul's neck and quickly closed the gap between them. Their mouths were already open when their lips contacted, tongues seeking entry, seeking each other. Their respective moans mingled in the still air of the bedroom as their hands wandered, grasping, groping, stroking. Hungry, urgent.

Palming Paul's cock, Kane revelled in how hot and hard it was beneath his touch, like the softest velvet wrapped around the most rigid steel, and he wondered if he could make the other man climax just by fucking his arse—with no stimulation on his cock whatsoever. It was time to find out.

"On your back." He wanted to watch Paul's face as they screwed, especially if Paul climaxed—it would be amazing.

Nodding, Paul rolled onto his back and bent his knees, spread his legs and presented Kane with easy access to his arsehole.

"Delicious," Kane growled, grabbing the bottle of lube and moving between Paul's thighs. He flipped open the cap, spread a liberal amount of liquid over his fingers, then reached down and circled Paul's hole. The other man gasped, flinched slightly, but didn't try to move away. In fact, he seemed to welcome the action, jerking his hips, encouraging Kane. It was fucking hot.

After squirting more liquid onto his digits, he began to work them inside Paul, stretching him and making the passage slippery. Finally, he smeared some onto his own shaft, making sure there was plenty on his bell end. Once he started, he didn't want to stop, not for anything. So he had to get it right first time, to ease the passage so he could sink inside the man in one fell swoop, possess him, fuck him.

He tossed the bottle aside, wiped his sticky hand on the duvet and crawled up so his and Paul's torsos were aligned and his cock was in position. Kane rocked his hips, sliding his shaft against Paul's balls and cock, tantalising them both, for a few seconds. Then he reached down and grasped the base of his dick, lined it up so the head pressed against Paul's ring. Then, glancing up at Paul's face for confirmation, he pushed inside. The other man bore down, making the initial resistance much less, entry much easier. Kane soon popped past the tight circle of muscle and was inside.

As he continued to push, Kane's eyes rolled back in his head as he was enveloped by an impossibly tight grip and a powerful sense of completion. He was sure it was something to do with the bite, with his animal side, but as he couldn't answer any of the questions that arose, he concentrated instead on the sensation.

Once he was balls-deep inside his lover, it didn't take long to lose himself. For as long as he could manage without driving himself insane, he pumped slowly in and out of Paul's back passage, each dragging motion pushing him closer to climax. He leaned down and captured the other man's lips in a heated kiss, one that made their already short breaths even more ragged. They moved in unison, as though they'd been doing this for years, as though they knew each other inside out and back to front. Paul reached up and tangled his hands in his lover's hair, pulled Kane harder onto his mouth, forcing their tongues deeper.

Kane gave Paul's bottom lip a sharp bite, a motion which wrenched a guttural groan from Paul and caused his cock to lurch, his body to bow, his arse to clench. Kane let out a feral growl and roughly shunted his hips. It was a chain reaction, each man's response driving the other crazy as they revelled in their mutual pleasure.

Soon, Kane could take it no more. His cock felt so hot and heavy it hurt, and he was holding onto his climax only through sheer bloody-mindedness. He needed to come, and he needed to come soon. After another long, deep, meaningful and toe-curling kiss, Kane ensured Paul was ready for him to up the ante. Then he began to thrust in and out of him, slowly at first, for as long as he could stand, then rapidly built up the speed until he felt his balls contract and shoot their contents up the length of his shaft and into Paul. Amazingly, Paul followed him into orgasm with a surprised howl, grunting and letting out a series of blasphemies before spunking ribbon after ribbon of cum all over his own stomach and chest.

Kane raised an eyebrow. He'd hoped, but hadn't been convinced it was possible for a man to come without his dick being touched. But then, it had been a day of surprises. And he was sure there were many more to come, for both of them.

He carefully pulled out, then went into the en suite to pee and wash up. That done, he grabbed a flannel, doused it in warm water and returned to the bedroom. After pressing a kiss to Paul's tousled hair, Kane cleaned his lover thoroughly and dropped the wet flannel onto the bedside cabinet. He could sort it later. Next, he dropped onto the mattress and opened his arms. Paul went into them willingly, with a satisfied sigh. Kane grinned widely, burying his face in the other man's hair and inhaling deeply. This was the start of something. He wasn't sure what, exactly, but he already knew for a fact it was going to be a wild ride.

Trespassing

Jack whistled cheerfully as he strode along one of the woodland paths on his father's estate. It'd be his estate one day, but he tried not to think about that. He was only twenty-two and nowhere near ready for that kind of responsibility and all the crap that went with it. His father, Gregory Hiddleston, was in the best of health and only in his forties himself, so it was easy for Jack to push it to the back of his mind. He'd worry about it when he absolutely had to, and not a moment before.

For now, he was enjoying the open space, the peace and quiet. It was a summer day so beautiful it was a cliché—the sky was blue, the sun bright and warm, sending beams of dappled light down onto him through the trees. Birds tweeted, called and sang, but otherwise there was silence. This part of the estate backed onto fields—also his father's, but there was public access through them—and as such, was far from any roads, tracks or anything else that would shatter the peace. It truly was idyllic and Jack paused, closed his eyes and let his head loll back. The sunshine bathed his face, the heat divine on his skin. Pulling in deep breaths, he smiled. Scents of nature; leaves, trees, undergrowth and dirt, assaulted his nostrils, added to the feelings of contentment. It was impossible to be anything but happy and grateful for such a blessed life on a gorgeous day like this.

For some moments, he continued to soak up the sun, half-wishing there was a bench nearby so he could fully relax without worrying about losing his balance and falling over. Not that there was anyone around to see him—the gamekeeper wasn't working today—but he'd still rather not sully his good mood by making an idiot of himself.

He was halfway through taking another deep breath when a sound reached his ears. A sound that didn't resemble anything he'd ever heard in nature. Not unless there was a very talented parrot loose in the woods that could talk and swear, anyway. He dropped his head to its normal position and opened his eyes.

More noise; rustling, grunting. A male voice. "Fucking hell, come out! For fuck's sake! Ow!"

Jack couldn't be sure as sound often travelled differently in the woods, but he thought the owner of the voice was ahead and to his left, close to the edge of the estate. His heart thumped, though he was sure it couldn't be a poacher—they wouldn't make that much noise and risk drawing attention to themselves, surely? Plus it was broad daylight and was well known in the area that the Hiddleston estate had a gamekeeper—and not so well known that there was only one such person, and therefore they did not work twenty-four hours a day, seven days a week.

Making his way towards the cursing trespasser, he wondered what he would find when he reached him. The grumbling and swearing grew louder, so it was obvious Jack was getting closer. Soon, he caught a glimpse of a horrible fluorescent colour through the trees—a high-vis vest or something, he guessed.

"Hello, who's there?" Jack called, injecting as much confidence into his voice as he could muster. Silly really that *he* was nervous, considering he was the only one out of the two of them who was *supposed* to be there.

"Oh, hello! Over here—can you help me, please?"

Relief coursed through Jack—whoever it was wasn't trying to hide or do anything dodgy, it seemed. They'd just got themselves into a predicament—albeit on private land.

When he rounded the next curve in the path, he quickly realised what had happened. The trespasser had apparently headed off the track for some reason—a call of nature, probably—and ended up sticking one of their feet into a crack in the ground. The man looked unhappy but relieved as Jack approached.

"Hello," he said, then pointed to his left leg and twisted his face into a grimace. "Can you help me, please? I was having a run and stopped to, um, relieve myself, but on the way back to the path I ended up getting my foot stuck in this damn hole. I can't budge it."

"Of course I can help," Jack said, squatting down next to the man, who appeared just a handful of years older than himself, and peering into the mass of undergrowth, roots and crumbled earth. He couldn't quite work out where the man's leg turned into ankle and then foot, so presumably he'd fallen quite deeply into the hole. "Do you mind?" He indicated the offending void in the earth.

"Go ahead. Thanks."

"Not a problem. Though I can't help but wonder why you were trespassing in the first place." He shoved a hand into the hole, then groped around until he found the man's ankle. The snarl-up was pretty bad—he'd have to dig him out.

"Trespassing?"

Jack quirked an eyebrow. "Yes. This is private land."

"So what are *you* doing here?" the man shot back.

"I live here. It's my father's land."

"Oh."

Well, that had shut him up. "Anyway, never mind that for now, you clearly weren't doing any harm. Except to yourself, apparently. You're wedged in pretty deep here. There's roots and leaves and God knows what else. Trying to pull you out could hurt your ankle or foot, if they're not damaged already. I'm going to head over to the gamekeeper's cottage and grab a spade or trowel or something, all right?"

"That would be great, thank you. I'm really sorry to inconvenience you. I honestly didn't know I was trespassing."

"Don't worry about that. I really am going to the gamekeeper's cottage to get something to dig you out. I'm not going to ring the police or anything. Just hang in there for a few minutes. It's not far."

"All right. Well, I'm not going anywhere." A feeble smile accompanied the man's attempt at humour, and Jack gave him what he hoped was a kind smile before turning and heading for the cottage.

He jogged along, aware that underneath all the dirt and leaves covering the man's lower leg could be a serious injury. He seemed more annoyed and embarrassed than in extreme pain, but it still paid to be cautious.

Once at the cottage, he knocked on the door. No response. He tried again. Nothing. Surmising no one was home, he retrieved the key from its hiding place on the windowsill behind a bunch of thick ivy and let himself in. Immediately, he made for the utility room at the back, hoping like hell he'd find something that would help. He didn't fancy trying to dig a hole with a spoon from the kitchen.

Fortunately, he quickly uncovered a trowel. It'd be slower going than a spade, but probably safer—the man's foot would have more chance of remaining attached to the rest of him, which he'd no doubt be pleased about.

He hurried out of the cottage and closed and locked the door, then pocketed the key. Once the accidental trespasser was freed, he'd bring him back here for a cup of tea and to check him over for injuries.

Garden tool in hand, he soon reached the spot where the man still sat miserably, most of his leg below the knee disappeared into the ground.

"I'm back," Jack said unnecessarily. "And I brought this. Between us, we'll get you out in no time."

"I hope you're right."

"I'm Jack, by the way. Jack Hiddleston."

"Ben Kiddell," the trespasser said. "My middle name is Very-Bloody-Embarrassed."

Jack let out a chuckle. "Don't be daft—happens to the best of us. Now, let's try and shift some of this crap so I can see what I'm doing. I don't want to end up stabbing you."

"Yeah, all right."

The two of them scrabbled around, pulled out clumps of leaves and sods of earth until they could see more clearly what had happened.

"Okay," Jack said, examining the area. "If you shift yourself and your foot as far over to your right as possible, I'll carefully chip away at this chunk of mud here and see if it helps. Crazy, isn't it—how the hell did you get your foot in that gap, and yet we can't get it out again?"

"God knows," Ben replied. "Perhaps a conspiracy by the woodland fairies or something. Maybe they were going to wait until dark then come out and eat me."

Jack shot Ben a glance. "Either you've regained your sense of humour or you're delirious. I've got enough to worry about, so I'm going to go with the former. Ready?"

Shuffling to his right, then leaning over as far as possible, Ben nodded. "When you are."

Feeling like an archaeologist, Jack scraped at the packed earth, getting considerably rougher when he got to areas full of plant roots. Force was the only way to deal with them and he caught the concerned look on Ben's face a couple of times when he started hacking away.

Before long, he'd got a good amount of the mud shifted. "Okay," he said, nodding at Ben, "give it a go now."

Ben shifted and carefully tried to pull his leg from the hole. It came out quite a way, but something still prevented him from being completely freed.

"Not to worry," Jack said, moving around the hole to get a better view of what still had a hold of Ben's foot. "I think I can see what the problem is—a stone or rock, I think. I'll chip away at the ground some more and hope it helps."

Jack's patience paid off when the rock fell from the dirt that had been holding it and deeper into the hole, freeing Ben's foot. He pulled his leg from the hole, then flopped onto his back and let out a whoop. "Thank God for that!" He sat up and looked at Jack. "Thanks, mate, I really appreciate your help. If I could just trespass for five more minutes, I'll get myself safely back on my feet and be on my way."

"Nonsense," Jack replied with a shake of his head. "We have no idea what damage has been done. I'll help you back to the gamekeeper's cottage and we'll check it out, all right? Then we can get you to a hospital or a doctor if needed."

"I'm all right, honestly." Ben slowly got to his feet, and Jack could see he was favouring the right leg, clearly wary of putting weight on the other one just yet. He waited until Ben tried it out, then hurried to his side as he winced.

"Come on, mate," he said, slipping his arm around Ben's back. "Put your arm around my shoulder and keep the weight off that foot. The cottage isn't far at all. Let's get you comfortable."

"Okay," Ben pouted. "I'm really sorry about all this. I genuinely have no idea how I ended up on private land."

The two began a slow journey through the woodland and towards the cottage. When they arrived, Jack encouraged Ben to lean up against the wall while he unlocked and opened the door. That done, he aided Ben across the threshold and into the sitting area. After helping Ben onto the sofa, he quickly grabbed all the cushions from the other sofa and chairs and piled them up at Ben's feet. "Get your trainer and sock off, if you can, and get your foot up here. I'll go and get some ice."

"Yeah, I can do that. Thanks."

Jack bustled off, closing the front door en route to the kitchen and wondering how his day had taken such a turn. One minute he'd been alone, enjoying the sunshine and the quiet. The next he'd been digging a stranger's foot out of a hole.

Now the panic was over and he had time to think about it, however, he came to the conclusion it wasn't all bad. Ben was actually pretty damn gorgeous, with his fluorescent vest thingy over the top of a white T-shirt and his navy blue running shorts. His light-gingery-coloured hair, damp with perspiration, flopped endearingly over his forehead, doing nothing to mask his sexy blue eyes. A generous mouth with a very pronounced cupid's bow begged kisses. And considerably naughtier things, too.

It was a good job he was reaching into the freezer for a bag of frozen peas. Slapping the bag briefly onto his crotch, he hoped it would take the heat out of the sudden erection he'd sprung. The last thing he wanted was to head back into the living room with his trousers tented and to scare the living daylights out of his patient. He was trying to help the guy, not traumatise him.

He closed the freezer, then stepped over to the worktop and flicked the kettle on, before grabbing a tea towel and walking back into the front room, where Ben had removed both his trainers and socks and had the good foot tucked beneath his other leg, while the injured one rested on the pile of cushions.

"How's it feeling?" Jack said, wrapping the bag of frozen peas in the tea towel and gently placing it on Ben's foot.

"Not too bad, to be honest. I've had a prod about and it's

definitely not broken. I don't think it's even a sprain. More of a twist and then a bit of crushing from the hole. There's no swelling, just a touch of redness. I reckon give it ten minutes and I'll be hunky-dory."

"Make it half an hour. I've just put the kettle on, and I'd rather be sure you're okay. Tea? Then you can tell me how you got into the woods—if there's a hole in the fencing somewhere or crap signage, I can let my dad know and we can get it sorted."

Ben huffed out a breath. "I'm—"

"*Please* don't apologise again. I'm not trying to make you feel guilty. I genuinely want to know. I'm a lot less territorial than the gamekeeper—if he'd found you, he probably would have kicked you off the land with a flea in your ear. And maybe his foot up your arse."

Ben gave a wry grin. "Tea would be great, thanks. Milk, two sugars."

"Is there any other way to take tea?" Jack tipped Ben a wink, then returned to the kettle just as it had finished boiling. He made the two cups of tea and went back to the living room. After handing Ben his mug, he lowered himself carefully into a chair, not wanting to spill the hot liquid.

"Thanks," Ben said, indicating the steaming drink.

"No problem."

They fell silent then, exchanging the odd smile as they blew and sipped at their drinks. Jack watched out of the corner of his eye as Ben peered around the room, taking in the contents, the decor, the architecture.

"Nice place," he eventually said. "If this is your gamekeeper's cottage, I'd love to see what the main house looks like."

Jack grinned. "I don't mean to brag, but it *is* pretty spectacular. But I suppose it's better to think that than to take it for granted."

"Absolutely. So, are you the oldest child?"

Realising immediately what Ben was getting at, Jack replied, "I'm the *only* child. So yes, unless something goes horribly wrong, I'll inherit Hiddleston House."

It seemed Ben hadn't expected such a perceptive answer. He raised his eyebrows. "Wow. Seems odd to me, but I guess for you it's totally normal."

"I'm afraid so. But to be honest, I'm not looking forward to all that."

"What, inheriting?"

"Yeah."

"Why not?"

Jack let out a heavy sigh, then took a sip of his tea. "It's... awkward."

"I'm sorry, I didn't mean to pry. I'm just interested."

"No, it's all right. I'm just not used to talking about it. Like, ever. I certainly can't tell my family, and most of my friends would either judge or blab."

"They don't sound like the best friends to have."

"They're not. But their parents and my parents are friends and blah-de-blah. It's just easier, keeps the peace—a quiet life and all that. I love it here, I really do, but it's much less stressful if I live for the day, the very moment, and don't worry or think about the future, because I know it's going to be tough."

"Inheriting gorgeous property and acres of land doesn't sound so tough. Surely you'll have staff to help you out."

"It's not that element I'm worried about. It's the... um... how should I put this? As the only child I'll inherit regardless, but it'll soon cause trouble when I don't produce any heirs."

Ben wrinkled his nose. "How do you know you won't produce any heirs? That's a bit defeatist!"

"I'm gay, Ben, that's why," Jack replied, deadpan.

"Oh. Shit. If my foot weren't propped up on your cushions, I'd remove it from my mouth." He paused, thinking. "God, I can see how difficult things will be, and it sucks. I take it if you adopted, had a surrogate or whatever, the child wouldn't be able to inherit?"

"I think if I had a child with a surrogate mother using my sperm, then the child could inherit. But Christ, I don't even know if I *want* kids yet. I'm young, single and haven't even come out yet. I've got a lot of bloody hurdles to jump before I even get to that stage."

"Now I totally understand why you live for the day and the moment. That's a lot of shit to carry around. If it makes you feel any better, the coming out bit isn't so hard. I sat my immediate family down in a room, plied them with a bit of booze, told them, then went out for a run and let them deal with it in their own way. By the time I came back—I should add I went for a *long* run—they'd clearly processed, talked about it amongst themselves and realised that deep down, they'd already known. Clearly, I'm not an aristocrat with property and inheritance to worry about, but my parents in particular are pretty conservative. Fortunately, they love me anyway. Do your folks love you?"

"Uh, I suppose so, yeah."

"Then it'll be fine. Have faith, and it'll be fine."

Jack huffed out a breath and ran his free hand through his hair. "How did my day turn into this? From solace and quiet to talking to a total stranger about surrogate mothers and coming out?"

Ben laughed, and Jack's heart gave a thump at the sound. At the way the mirth transformed Ben's face, his eyes crinkling at the corners, dancing with amusement, and dimples appearing in his cheeks.

"Life's weird like that. You have to embrace it."

"And what are the sodding chances of a trespasser on my future land being gay, too?"

Shrugging, Ben said, "I dunno. Maybe it's fate. Maybe we were meant to meet."

Jack stared at him. "Did you hit your head, too?"

Ben stuck his tongue out before draining his tea, reaching over to slide a coaster across the table and putting his empty mug down on it. "No, I didn't. I'm just being practical. I got here by accident. You were walking by yourself, not expecting to see anyone. Our paths crossed, and it's clear you needed to talk to someone about this. And here I am. It wasn't planned, so it's either pure coincidence, or fate. Whatever you want to call it, it's a good thing."

"How's hurting yourself a good thing?"

"Well, it's not. I meant my being here, lending an ear. Do you feel better having got stuff off your chest?"

Jack thought for a moment. "Yeah, I do, actually. Thank you. It was good to get it out there, even though I don't have any answers."

"You're welcome. And you know what they say, a problem shared is a problem halved."

Jack put his drink down, then stood and moved to the end of Ben's sofa. "Okay, let's get those peas off you and look at the ankle, shall we?"

"Is that a come on?"

Jack spluttered. "What? What gave you that idea?"

Ben's grin was wide. "Jack. Calm down. I'm teasing you."

"Oh." Heat flamed up his throat and across his cheeks. "Sorry." He grabbed the tea towel-covered bag of peas and the two empty mugs and all but ran to the kitchen.

After returning the frozen goods to their rightful place, he set about washing up the crockery, drying it and putting it away. He'd never hear the end of it if he left them lying around for Clive to find whenever he got back from whatever he did on his day off. He'd retrieve the trowel and put that back where he'd found it, too.

He'd just closed the cupboard door and put the tea towel on its hook when he sensed a presence behind him. Whirling, he opened his mouth to tell Ben off. "What are you doing upright? You should still be lying down!"

Ben laughed. "Now who's coming on to whom?"

Scowling, Jack shot back, "Stop trying to embarrass me and

go and get your feet back up."

"Christ, you're bossy. I'm fine, look." To prove his point, Ben walked around the kitchen without limping, wobbling or wincing. "It was just a twist. Nothing to worry about."

"Huh. Okay. Well that's good then. In that case, are you up for showing me how you got onto the property? I can report back then and make sure the problem gets fixed."

Ben walked back over to him before stopping barely a pace away. "What's the rush? Do you have somewhere better to be?"

Jack's heart rate picked up. Heat flared in his groin, threatening to make his erection reappear. "N-no. It's just..."

"Just what?" Moving closer still, Ben tucked Jack's hair behind his ears. Jack dropped his gaze to the floor. "Come on, posh boy, what's the problem? I like you. I *think* you like me. Why not take advantage of this coincidence, fate, or whatever the bloody hell it is and have some fun?"

"I don't know..." Jack bit his lip.

"*Do* you like me, Jack? Or have I read the signs totally wrong?"

Jack sighed. "I do like you. I do. I just don't know... what I'm doing. You know... having sex with a man." He lifted his head, met Ben's gaze. "I've never done it before. Not even a kiss."

"Well," Ben grinned. "I think we can fix that, can't we?" After shuffling forward until Jack's body was trapped between him and the kitchen cupboards, he leaned down and pressed his lips to the younger man's.

Jack's mind raced. He was glued to the spot for several long moments until Ben's tongue sought access to his mouth. Something clicked then, and he responded, not really knowing how but trying to trust his instincts. He moved his arms from his sides, slipped them around Ben and clasped his hands together in the small of Ben's back. Then he opened his mouth, tentatively poked out his own tongue to explore, gauging the rhythm from the more experienced man and going along with it. It felt good, so good, and he soon relaxed, his brain shutting off and his body taking over.

By the time Ben pulled away, a look of intense desire in his eyes, Jack was so horny he thought he might explode. His cock threatened to rip out of the confines of his clothes, and his balls were ready to empty their load.

His voice low, husky, Ben said, "Do you want to go upstairs? I'm guessing there's a spare room in here—I have no desire to fuck you on the gamekeeper's bed!"

Jack let out a squeak. "Fuck? B-but we don't have any condoms, or lube, or—"

Ben cut him off by pressing a finger to his lips. "Shush. Stop panicking. For one thing, I'm not going to make you do anything you don't want to do, or aren't ready for. Plus, there are lots of things we can do without needing condoms or lube..." He gave a wolfish smirk, one that sent a fresh bolt of lust to Jack's nether regions and almost made him come right there and then, in his boxers. *Yeah, because that wouldn't be embarrassing at all.*

"Oh." He coughed. "Okay then." Trying, but failing miserably, to sound calmer, he said, "Yes, there's a spare room. Want to go up?"

"Do I ever! But do you?" The older man's expression was now completely serious, his eyes kind, but with arousal still flickering in the background.

"Yes," he stated. "Yes, I do. Let's go and do whatever we can do without needing condoms or lube." He grabbed Ben's hand, led him from the kitchen and out into the hallway, then up the creaking staircase, secretly sending up pleas to any gods that might be listening to stop Clive from coming home any time soon. *Because that wouldn't be totally embarrassing, either.*

They entered the spare bedroom, then parted briefly while Jack closed and locked the door, then crossed to the window and drew the curtains. He laughed as he did so. "I have no idea why I'm doing this. Only bloody birds can see us! Maybe squirrels."

Instead of replying, Ben pulled off his hi-vis vest and T-shirt, before dropping them to the carpet. They were quickly joined by his shorts and boxers, and Jack couldn't prevent his gaze from dropping to the other man's cock. His own throbbed almost painfully, and his mouth watered. He wanted to taste that cock, to touch it, to feel its hardness and its heat...

Ben sat on the double bed, then scooted up to rest on the pillows. He beckoned. "Get naked and come here."

After grabbing his nervousness, screwing it up and shoving it to the very back of his mind, Jack did just that. As Ben pulled him gently into his arms and began kissing him again, he knew he had nothing to worry about. He was in good hands.

Their bodies pressed together, cocks brushing against each other, straining, leaking precum, eager to be touched. But there was no rush—right now, kissing was all that mattered. Parted lips, heaving chests, thrusting tongues... Jack had never experienced anything like it before in his life, and already he knew he was going to get addicted.

Gaining a little confidence, Jack let his hands wander. He tangled them in Ben's hair, cupped his face, stroked his throat, his pecs, the ridges of his abdomen. Exploring further, he reached around and cupped a pert buttock, the skin smooth, but the muscle beneath firm and ripe.

Soon, he could hold back no longer. He wanted more; had to have more. He shifted his hand to the front of Ben's body and hesitantly gripped his shaft, trying to tell himself that he'd touched his own cock enough times—this was the same, but on another person. With that in mind he brushed his thumb across the tip, broke their kiss and brought his hand briefly to his mouth to suck off the precum, then carried on with what he'd been doing. Their mouths collided once more as he closed his fist around Ben's dick, finding the grip and position that worked best, marvelling at the sensation of steel wrapped in warm velvet beneath his fingers. Satisfied, he began to masturbate Ben, paying attention to the sounds he made, to the tension in his body. He wanted to arouse him, give him pleasure, but not make him come. Not just yet—he was reserving that until a little later, until he sunk his mouth onto the other man's cock and sucked him dry.

The mere thought drove him crazy, so when Ben reached out and mirrored his movements, grasping his shaft and tossing him off, Jack pulled away from their kiss and let out a yowl. "Stop, you'll make me come!"

Ben chuckled. "Isn't that kind of the point?"

"It is, but not yet. I want to make you come."

"And I want to make you come. Why can't we do it together?"

"Because I want to swallow your cum."

Ben raised an eyebrow. "That's brave for a first timer."

Shrugging, Jack said, "What can I say? As soon as I saw your cock, I wanted to taste it."

"Well, that can be arranged." He pulled away and shifted on the bed.

"Hey, what are you doing?"

"Wait and see."

It didn't take long for even Jack's naive brain to work out what was going on when Ben's cock appeared in front of his face. "Ah. Okay. Good idea."

"All right with this?" Ben said, grinning up at him from crotch level. Or was that grinning down?

Ben's hot breath on Jack's dick made him shiver with delight. "Oh yeah. More than all right."

There was nothing more to be said, so, after exchanging a heat-filled glance, the two of them got to work. Jack quickly realised it was hard to concentrate on giving head—especially for the first time—when someone was also sucking you off, but he did his best. He seemed to be doing the trick, too, as Ben's shaft swelled and lengthened in his mouth, and the moans the other man made vibrated up his own cock, making him groan. It was like a vicious circle, only good. Perfect, actually.

Before long, Jack felt like he'd been sucking cock forever. And he really fucking liked it. It felt good, tasted great, and the feeling of power, of gratification when Ben suddenly thrust his hips hard and began to climax was mind-blowing. So mind-blowing it triggered his own orgasm; a long, drawn-out period of total bliss and satisfaction that made him want to drag Ben back to the main house and lock him in his room until they were both fucked out.

As their cocks softened, a lethargic Ben turned around the right way on the bed and flopped down next to him. They kissed again, gently, intimately, the taste of their mutual pleasure exploding over their taste buds. Pulling away, Jack grinned at his lover and shoved his hair back from his forehead, the better to look into his eyes. "You know what? You should totally trespass on this land more often."

Ben twisted his head and kissed Jack's palm. "You know what? I totally intend to."

An Interesting Find
Chapter One

Nathan closed his book with a very final slap and put it on the coffee table in front of him, then leaned back in his chair. Stretching languidly, he said, "Bloody good, that was. Though, admittedly, I thought it'd last me all week. Wasn't expecting to get through it on day one."

Raising an eyebrow, Lee shot Nathan an amused glance. "Not far off myself. Fucking storm. Stupid us, eh, going on holiday in the UK in summertime—not like you can guarantee the sodding weather, is it? Should've gone to the Canaries."

"No, we can't guarantee the weather, but..." Nathan gave the window a sidelong glance, "I do have some good news."

"Yeah?"

"Yeah. The torrential downpour has stopped."

"Seriously?" Lee slammed his own book closed and scurried over to the window. "Oh, wow, it's cleared right up, and I can see a rainbow. Wanna head out? Just a little wander down to that pond we saw on the way here, maybe? Get some fresh air. We've got loads of daylight left, haven't we?"

Nathan checked his watch. "Plenty. Especially if we're only nipping to the pond. It's probably only a fifteen-minute walk."

"Fantastic. I was going a bit stir crazy in here. I'll grab our coats and shoes."

Lee had disappeared into the hallway of their rented holiday cottage before Nathan had the chance to reply. Shaking his head with a smile, Nathan collected their empty mugs from the coffee table and took them into the kitchen, then got a bottle of water from the fridge. He doubted they'd need a drink during their short trek along the road, but he could just shove the bottle in his coat pocket and forget about it. At least it'd be there if they wanted it.

When he returned to the living room, Lee was just about to tie up his laces.

"I got water," Nathan said, brandishing the bottle.

"Cool. Shoes are there." He nodded to the chair Nathan had been sitting in. Sure enough, his trail shoes were waiting on the floor in front of it.

"Thanks."

Within a few minutes, they were headed out of the door. Nathan locked up, pocketed the key, then checked the handle. He doubted very much the place would get broken into—they were in the middle of nowhere, after all. There were farms nearby, but the closest village was about a mile and a half away. So any thieves would have to make a considerable effort to get to the cottage in the first place, never mind attempt to break into it. Rolling his eyes at his own paranoia, he turned and followed Lee, who'd already started ambling along the road in the direction of the pond.

After falling into step beside Lee, Nathan pulled in some deep breaths, enjoying the fresh air after being cooped up in the cottage. It was beautiful, and cosy, but it was supposed to be a base for them to go walking—somewhere for them to eat, sleep and shower, not to be stuck in for hours on end, staring at the walls. Or climbing them.

He admired the rainbow as they walked, its vivid colours painted across the watery sky. It seemed the clouds had literally exhausted themselves—only occasional wispy streaks of white now interrupted the never-ending blue. The sun beamed down, heating up the ground and beginning to evaporate the huge puddles. It would take some doing—one such puddle stretched across the width of the road, and they had to skirt around its edge to avoid getting wet feet.

Nathan smiled. Though the storm itself had been grim, the washed-out aftermath made everything feel fresh, clean somehow.

"You look thoughtful," Lee said, breaking into his reverie. "A penny for them?"

"Mmm. It's one of those things that sounds better in your head than said out loud."

"Try me."

Shrugging, Nathan replied, "Nothing major. Just admiring the rainbow, the sky, the clouds… thinking how everything looks so fresh and clean after a good storm. Like it's been purified or something… Ugh, it's stupid."

Lee stopped and reached for Nathan's hand. His green eyes were wide and filled with wonder. "No, it isn't. Not at all—I was thinking something similar myself. It's kinda romantic, isn't it? Purification, rebirth, and all that."

"In a roundabout way, maybe. I dunno." He shrugged again.

Lee's eyes narrowed, and his lips curved into a wicked grin. "We could *make* it romantic."

"How so?"

"Come here and I'll show you." Still gripping Nathan's hand,

Lee tugged him close and moved in for a kiss. Nathan went into the embrace willingly, the smile on his face soon smothered by Lee's hot lips.

Twining their arms around each other, they deepened their kiss. Mouths opening, tongues searching, stubble scratching. Nathan moaned, tucking his hands under the back of Lee's waterproof coat and gripping his firm, muscular arse cheeks. Arse cheeks he'd parted a thousand times, exploring between them with fingers, tongue, cock…

His head swum with erotic images, and he suddenly wished more than anything they were back at the cottage so they could take things further. Oh, the irony—they'd been in the place all bloody day, eager to leave, and now they'd left, he wanted to return.

Reluctantly, he broke the kiss. "Phew." He blinked rapidly, trying to regain his equilibrium. Blood and adrenaline rushed around his body, making him a little unsteady. "That was… intense."

"And romantic." Lee grinned, the mischief and arousal in his eyes blatant.

"Yeah, all right." Nathan mirrored the grin. "It *was* romantic. But we'd better carry on walking, otherwise romantic is rapidly going to turn erotic, and no matter how remote this road is, I don't think taking our clothes off here is a good idea."

"You're probably right." He briefly tightened his grip on Nathan's hips. "But this is to be continued later, okay?"

"You'll get no arguments from me."

"Good." After dropping a much more chaste kiss on Nathan's lips, Lee released him and took his hand again. "Now let's get moving, before I change my mind."

Nathan chuckled as they turned and continued walking along the quiet road, with nothing but the sights and sounds of nature around them, the moorland stretching for miles in each direction. He sighed happily—what could be better than this? A beautiful location, fantastic company, some rest and relaxation—that was what this trip was supposed to be about. The fact their first day had been mostly written off by shitty weather had made him forget all that. But he'd been reminded now, and he was going to make the most of it, the most of his time with Lee. At home, they didn't get a lot of alone time—they both had busy careers, and Lee worked shifts, so sometimes they didn't see each other properly for days. Now they had a solid, uninterrupted week together, and it was going to be blissful.

Soon, their destination came into view, and they crossed the road again, then walked a little way along a track, before heading off it and down into the dip that held the pond.

"Wow," Lee said, letting gravity carry him the rest of the way down the slope. He came to a stop beside a bench. "This is cool. Right next to a road, and yet it feels so remote." Glancing around, he added, "It's kinda eerie, actually."

"Yeah," Nathan replied, joining him, "I know what you mean. If you ignore the bench, there's such little evidence of man. Someone could send us back in time a hundred, a thousand years, and I reckon this place would look pretty much the same."

"Nice to be reminded there are still lots of unspoilt places left in this country, isn't it?"

"It is. Come on, let's sit. Our coats should be long enough to keep our bums dry. If not, a damp bum never killed anyone, did it?"

"Nah." Lee tugged at the bottom of his coat, trying to cover his rear, then sat. "I promise to warm your bum up if it gets cold, though."

"You're too kind." Nathan shot his lover an amused glance as he took a seat. "Likewise."

They lapsed into silence then, contentedly admiring the world around them—the craggy steel-grey hills in the distance, the undulating grass and moorland between, the steep banks either side of them, and the dark, spooky body of water behind them. Nathan turned one hundred and eighty degrees on the bench to get a better look. It really *was* spooky—the surface of the pool was completely flat, undisturbed. As though it was utterly devoid of life. He suppressed a shudder, not wanting Lee to take the piss out of him and his often-vivid imagination.

Something that didn't look quite right drew his gaze. Focusing hard on the area on the other side of the pond, he tried to figure out what exactly he was seeing—if anything. The more he looked, the more he was convinced there was something at the bottom of the sheer slope leading up to the road—not that one could tell that from here.

"Um, Lee?" he finally said, unable to ignore his instincts any longer.

"Yeah?"

Nathan pointed. "Does something over there look… not quite right to you?"

Lee swivelled on the bench. "Where—*Oh.* Shit. Is that what I think it is?"

"I dunno. What do you think it is?"

"Looks like a person to me. In camouflage gear." Lee's eyes were wide, his expression panicked.

Nathan jumped up, exhaling a heavy breath. "Oh, thank fuck for that. I thought it was just me."

"Nope." Lee got up too. All thoughts of bums, damp or otherwise, had been completely forgotten. "Let's go and see. I really hope we're not about to find something awful."

"Me too."

Quickly but cautiously, they made their way around the pond, careful to avoid the boggy areas surrounding it. The last thing they needed was a twisted ankle, or worse. Especially not when it appeared someone might need their help.

When they were just a handful of steps away, Nathan turned to Lee, his mouth suddenly dry. "Should we call an ambulance?"

Lee shook his head. "Not yet. Not until we know for sure what's happening. It could be a bundle of rags. We'd look stupid then. Not to mention wasting their time."

"True." Somehow, he knew it wasn't a bundle of rags, but his racing heart was happy for him to keep up the pretence for a few seconds more.

Together, Nathan and Lee closed the gap between themselves and the mysterious person or object.

Chapter Two

"Oh, Christ," Lee said, standing over the bundle. "It's a man!"

"Really? Oh my God! Is he breathing? Has he got a pulse? And what the fuck is he doing here? Did someone kill him?"

Lee turned away from the man, put his hands on Nathan's shoulders and shook them a little. "Hey, get a grip. You're no good to me—or him—babbling like this. I don't know the answers to any of those questions yet. Just calm the fuck down and let me find out, all right? And phone an ambulance!" He spun back to face the camouflaged figure and dropped to his knees on the rough grass, reaching out a tentative hand to search for a pulse.

Fighting to get a handle on his fear and panic, Nathan started rooting through his pockets for his phone. Ambulance—Lee had said to call for an ambulance. Yes, that was sensible. After a fruitless search, he swallowed hard. "Uh, Lee?"

"Yeah?" He didn't turn around, just kept doing whatever he was doing to the man.

"I, uh, haven't got my phone on me. Can I use yours?"

Lee peered at him then, a wry expression on his face. "Fuck. I haven't got mine either. But on a lighter note, this guy has a pulse. It's a little slow, but it's there, thank God. He's breathing, but unconscious. And he's wet through and freezing cold. We need to get him inside, fast. Can you run and get the car? It'll be quicker and safer than us trying to carry him back to the cottage."

"Yes, of course. See you in a few." Nathan half turned away, then spun back as a thought occurred to him. "Oh, here. Take this water in case he wakes up."

Taking the proffered bottle, Lee replied, "Good idea. Thanks. See you soon. Hurry!"

"Hurrying!" Nathan clambered up the slope, picking up speed as he hit the level. Then, when he was on the flatter surface of the road, he began to run—this time not bothering to avoid the puddles. Wet feet hardly mattered when a man's life was on the line.

The run seemed to clear his mind, so by the time he got to the cottage he was much more focused. Quickly, he let himself into the building and searched for his phone. Since they'd arrived on their break he'd not really given it a second thought—the whole point of being on holiday was to get away from everything.

He finally spotted the device on his bedside table and grabbed it. No signal. *Fucking typical!*

Lee's phone. Where was it? Renewing his search, he soon located Lee's phone on the other bedside table. It was on a different network from his, so perhaps he'd have a signal.

Fuck it! Still nothing. Resisting the temptation to throw the phones at the wall, he instead threw them onto the bed, breathing hard. The bed gave him a thought.

He rushed into the second bedroom, pulled the blanket and duvet off the bed and bundled them up into his arms. Then he grabbed his car keys from the coffee table and ran back out of the cottage, this time not bothering to lock the door behind him. It'd just slow them down when they came back, and he didn't have time to worry about thieves right now.

Within a minute, he'd shoved the bedding into the back seat

of the car, jumped in, started the engine and zoomed out of the parking area behind the cottage. He steered the vehicle onto the road, then drove as fast as he dared along it—it was no good him going so fast he crashed. They'd be even more screwed then.

Unsurprisingly, on the short journey he didn't pass a single person, either on foot or in a vehicle. Not a soul to help him, help them. For now at least, the mystery man's survival was down to him and Lee.

I hope the poor bloke's strong, otherwise his chances with us are minimal.

He beeped the car's horn as he pulled onto the track, hoping Lee would realise it was him signalling his return. Then, eager to save time, he turned the car around so it was facing the road again. Leaving the engine running, he jumped out, opened the rear door and grabbed the bedding.

"Lee!" he called, hurrying back down towards the pond. "I've got some blankets to wrap him up in. I know dry clothes would be better, but I was trying to be quick."

"It's fine," Lee said, holding out his arms for the bundle, then taking it the moment Nathan reached him. "Good thinking. He's still the same. Haven't had a peep out of him, unfortunately. Is the ambulance on its way?" As he spoke, he opened the duvet out on the grass next to the man, but left the blanket to one side. He now looked much more like a man, as Lee had laid him out flat. He wasn't just a bundle of camo rags anymore—he had a head, and arms and legs. Everything seemed to be where it should be.

"Um, about that…"

Lee gave him a sharp glance.

Nathan shrugged, his hands spread wide. "I'm sorry, all right? Neither of our phones have a signal, and I haven't seen a landline phone in the cottage."

"Fuck. Never mind that for now. We need to hurry. Get by his feet. We'll lift him onto the duvet, and put the blanket over him. I thought we could use the duvet as a makeshift stretcher. Not ideal, I know, but better than leaving the poor bastard out here, especially if there's no ambulance coming."

"It's not my fault," Nathan shot back, doing as he was told.

"I'm not blaming you. I'm just saying. Okay, right. Are you ready?"

Nathan nodded, gripping the man's ankles.

"On the count of three. One... two... *three*!"

After carefully lifting their charge onto the duvet and covering him with the blanket, they took the corners of their rudimentary stretcher and began carefully but quickly making their way up the bank to the car.

Once there, Nathan asked, "So, how are we going to get him in the back?"

"Uh..." Lee was silent for a couple of seconds, then he said, "Right, put him down a minute, and go and open the other back door. Then you come around and shuffle backwards into the car, pulling him with you. Get out the other side and shut the door. Does that make sense?"

"Yeah."

It was more difficult in reality than it was verbally, but after a great deal of manoeuvring and grunting and groaning, the two men finally got the unconscious stranger into the back of their car.

"Fucking hell," Nathan said as he slid behind the wheel and closed the door. Lee was just getting in the other side. "In a way, it's a good job no one was around to see that, otherwise it'd have looked like we were putting a dead body in our car or something." After glancing over to make sure Lee was safely in the vehicle, he put the car in gear, released the handbrake and started driving back to the cottage.

Lee snorted, then glanced worriedly over his shoulder into the back of the car. "I hope we weren't putting a dead body in the fucking car. Besides, if anyone did see us, surely they'd realise we were doing it all wrong. I would think someone trying to hide a dead body would take it *out* of their car—most likely the boot—and dump it in a deserted spot in the countryside, not the other way around!"

Nathan shook his head. "We'd be the worst murderers ever."

"Yes, we would. So let's stick to saving this guy, eh?"

The journey back to the cottage must have taken only a few minutes, but to Nathan it felt like hours. They'd been in such a rush to help the man that he hadn't got a proper look at him, but even the briefest of glances showed the situation was far from good. The guy was in real danger, and the prospect scared the crap out of him.

Nathan pulled the car up next to the front door. "I'll move it once he's settled. I'm hardly going to cause traffic issues out here, am I?"

"Okay. Let's go."

With an awkward reverse re-enactment, somehow they

moved their patient out of the car and into the cottage, thankful it was single story. Getting the man up a flight of stairs would have been nigh on impossible.

They carefully lowered him onto the bed in the second bedroom. Lee set about removing his heavy-duty boots.

"So," Nathan said, moving over to close the curtains, though the moment he did he realised how pointless the exercise was. There was nobody around to see in the damn window, anyway. "What's the plan now?"

"I suppose…" Lee dropped one of the boots to the floor with a thud. "We should take his clothes off. Feels a bit fucking weird, but I don't see what choice we've got. He's probably got hyperthermia, so we need to get him warmed up. I think if he could speak—given the choice between dying and having two strangers take his clothes off, he'd probably choose the latter. I know I would." The other boot thumped onto the carpet.

"Yeah, you're right. Shall I go and run a hot bath?"

"Uh…" Lee scratched his head and screwed his eyes shut. "No. Let me think. Fuck's sake, we've got no signal, and we deliberately chose a cottage without Wi-Fi, so I can't bloody Google it. I can't remember what the dos and don'ts are for hyperthermia. I'm wondering if it might be a good idea to nip to the nearest farm and see if they've got a phone we can use. They're bound to have a landline. Hospital's gotta be the best place for this guy."

"N-no. No hospitals." The voice was weak, but the intention behind the words was resolute.

"Fucking hell! Scared the shit out of me." Lee clutched his

chest, then scurried to the head of the bed. "Mate, can you hear me? You're safe with us, we're going to look after you. Can you tell us your name, and what happened?"

"No hospitals."

Lee glanced at Nathan, who shrugged. "All right, if you say so. No hospitals. Don't bloody die on us then, will you?"

"W-won't die. Just… need to get warm."

"Yes, that's right. That's what we were going to do. We think you might have hyperthermia, mate."

"Hy*po*thermia."

"Yeah, that's what I said."

"Didn't. Different."

"All right, all right." Lee's expression was tight. "So, you sound like you know what you're talking about. Am I right in thinking we take your clothes off and warm you slowly?"

"Y-yes. And a warm drink."

Finally! Nathan zipped into the kitchen and set about making three cups of tea. Wouldn't hurt for him and Lee to have one, too.

Happier now he felt useful, he filled and flicked on the kettle, then, knowing the thing took an age to boil, ran outside to move the car around the back. It didn't seem as though they'd be needing it any time soon, not if their new friend was adamant he didn't want to go to hospital.

But the question remained—why the hell not?

Chapter Three

When Nathan returned to the spare bedroom, he saw their unexpected guest was now wrapped up like the oddest kind of mummy. Even his face was barely visible from within the bulk of duvets, blankets and pillows.

Lee was just heading out of the door with the bundle of wet camouflage gear. "I'm just gonna go hang this stuff in the drying room."

"All right." Nathan nodded. "Let me just put these mugs down and I'll bring the boots in, too."

"Okay, thanks."

Nathan walked towards the bed, then carefully put the tray down on the bedside cabinet. Looking over, he saw the man peering back at him through slitted eyes. "Hey," he said gently, "I hope you're starting to warm up in there. Lee's taken your clothes to start drying them. I'm just going to take your boots, too, then we'll be back. We'll get you sitting up so you can have a drink, all right?"

A barely perceptible nod.

Nathan grabbed the boots, then headed for the drying room.

"Hey," he said when he entered.

Lee glanced over his shoulder with a smile. He was just placing the last item of clothing on the drying rack. "Hey. He okay?"

Nathan stepped forward to place the boots next to the radiator. "Seems to be. From what I can tell under all those layers, he's getting a little more colour in his face. I told him we were just sorting his clothes, then we'd be back to help him sit up and have a drink."

"What did he say?"

"Bugger all. Just sort of nodded."

Lee screwed up his face. "Hmm." Then, quietly pulling the door closed behind them, he continued, "Is it me, or do you think there's something a bit weird going on here? I mean, the poor bloke is unquestionably ill, but why the hell is he so dead set against going to hospital? He hasn't managed to tell us his name, what happened, or anything. All we know is he doesn't want to go to hospital. God…" He paled. "You don't think we've picked up a criminal or something, do you?"

Nathan's heart lurched as he considered the possibilities. They'd been off the grid since arriving at the cottage, so there could be a manhunt going on in the area for all they knew. Mind you… "Uh, no, I don't think so. Surely if there was something going on, we'd have heard sirens, helicopters, search parties…"

"They could have been called off because of the storm."

"True. But it's gorgeous out there now, they'd be back out. Besides, he was in camo gear. Are we ignoring the obvious here? He's a soldier."

"You don't have to be a soldier to wear camo gear."

"Also true. But there is a military training area around here somewhere. I saw it on the OS map."

"Oh." Lee pursed his lips thoughtfully. "Then we could have our answer. Except he's not wearing any dog tags."

"Do all soldiers have to wear dog tags, all of the time?"

"I don't bloody know. I'm an engineer, not a soldier."

Nathan stuck out his tongue. "All right, arsey. I'm just trying to figure things out. So all we have is a freezing cold man and a potential army uniform. No dog tags, no form of ID, no bag, no nothing… Fuck, I hope we can get him talking once he's feeling more up to it."

"Yeah," Lee sighed, opening the door, "me too."

They made their way back to their patient, who didn't appear to have moved an inch. "We're back," Nathan said unnecessarily. "Ready for something to drink?"

"Yes, please," the voice came, a little stronger this time.

Thank God—looks like he's on the mend, after all.

Without another word, Nathan and Lee shifted to opposite sides of the bed and knelt on the mattress either side of the other man. "All right?" Lee said to Nathan.

"Yep. Can you lift him, and I'll pile up pillows behind him?"

"Sure. Ready? On three. One… two… *three*."

Their task went without a hitch, and now their mummified man was in a position to have a drink. Nathan frowned as he considered him. Trouble was, given only his face was exposed, it might not be that easy.

Shuffling off the bed, he said, "Be right back!" and headed for the kitchen. He'd seen something earlier. At the time he'd thought it stupid, but now he realised it could just be the very thing he needed most right now. Aside from a miracle, that was.

He opened the utensil drawer, grabbed the pink, curly straw with a grimace—not like the mystery man could afford to be picky right now—and returned to the bedroom, holding it aloft. "Problem solved."

Lee regarded the straw, then sniggered. "Not very masculine, but hey-ho. Better than dehydration on top of everything else. Good idea—I hadn't thought of that."

After returning to sit beside their patient, Nathan carefully picked up the cup of tea and put the straw in the mug. Then he turned and held it to the man's lips, idly wondering if the hot liquid would melt the plastic straw. Hopefully not.

The man looked down, going a little cross-eyed in the process, then slowly opened his lips enough to admit the straw. After a moment the tea zipped up the translucent tube and the level in the mug began rapidly decreasing. Nathan held back a sigh of relief—if this guy was sitting up and drinking, and had been talking a little, then before long he should be able to tell them his name and what had happened to him. He bloody well hoped so, anyway. The questions, the worries whizzing around Nathan's mind were making him anxious.

A couple of minutes later, their patient turned his head away, the straw popping out of his mouth as he did so. He gulped, then said, "Thank you." His voice was still quiet, still husky, but stronger. There was definitely a healthier glow in his cheeks, too.

"You're welcome," Nathan said with a smile, putting the now-empty mug down and picking up his own and Lee's before handing the latter over to him.

"Glad you're feeling a bit better," Lee added, then took a sip of his own drink. "Mmm… good tea, as always, Nathan. Thanks."

Nathan grinned by way of reply, wondering how he could get the man beside him to talk. He had a feeling that the more they pushed, the more he'd clam up. Or possibly even flat-out lie to them.

He pondered as he sipped at his tea, trying not to linger on the awkward silence that had now fallen. It was hardly surprising, though, given the circumstances. It wasn't often someone was rescued from potential death out in the elements, and *wasn't* taken to hospital. This part would normally be taken care of by medical professionals, people who knew what they were doing, people who had good bedside manners and liked taking care of others.

He and Lee, on the other hand, just about muddled through taking care of themselves. They didn't even have so much as a pet goldfish or a house plant. And now, here they were, being forced to look after a real, live human being. Really, it was a wonder the bloke had made it this far. Probably only because he'd known what to do and had told them. Otherwise they might have finished him off by doing the wrong thing.

Nathan drained his mug, then stood. "Okay, I'm going to rustle up some food. Lee, you want something?" Then, before he could stop himself, he turned to their patient. "What about you, mystery man? Would you like something to eat? I can do a sandwich, some soup… Nothing too fancy, I'm afraid. We were planning on eating out tonight."

The man narrowed his eyes. "Yes, please. Maybe soup and some bread?"

"Coming right up." The chipper tone was fake, but he hoped it wasn't too obvious. Lee would have clocked it, he was sure, but he'd also know *why* he was pissed off. "Lee?"

"I'll come and help you," he replied, getting up. Together,

they left the room and went into the kitchen.

Putting his and the stranger's mug down on the draining board, Nathan let out a little growl of frustration. Then, keeping his voice low, said, "I don't like this, Lee. That time, he was *deliberately* not giving his name. He knew exactly what I was getting at, and could easily have volunteered the information, but chose not to. And I want to know *why*. God, if he's dodgy, he could murder us both as soon as he's feeling better. Murder us, rob us, then take off in the car and no one would ever know what happened to us."

Lee sighed, placing his own mug beside the others. He ran a hand through his hair. "I'm inclined to agree. The first time he didn't volunteer the information, I gave him the benefit of the doubt because he's seriously poorly. He could have been out of it, or maybe not *remember* who he was, or something. Now, though, I'm confident it's deliberate. I say we feed the bloke, then give him one last chance. If he won't tell us what the fuck is going on, then we threaten to take him to hospital or phone the police. He's got to move on at some point—this is only a bloody holiday cottage, he can't stay here forever. I think the owners would have something to say about it, don't you?"

"Yeah. He might give whoever's renting this place next week a bit of a fright. I can imagine the owners now: 'Oh, yes, we just found him here, and he's refusing to leave. We've decided to keep him. He adds character to the place. Like some kind of pet. Look after him for us, would you?'"

Lee let out a laugh, then moved over and pulled Nathan into

a hug. They embraced for a few seconds, squeezing tightly, taking comfort and solace from each other without having to say another word. Lee gave Nathan a quick kiss, then released him. "Come on, let's get this food sorted. The sooner we feed him, the sooner we can get to the bottom of this one way or the other, all right? Everything's going to be okay. You know that, don't you?"

Nodding, Nathan turned to the cupboards and searched for a saucepan. "Soon is good for me. We're supposed to be on holiday to relax, not to take in random strays and look after them. We could have stayed at home and done that!"

Chapter Four

Between them, Nathan and Lee put together a basic meal of ham and cheese sandwiches, soup, and bread, as well as another three cups of tea. They carried the goodies through to the spare bedroom.

Apparently feeling stronger now, the mystery man had wrestled his arms out of the material covering him. Relief washed over Nathan—at least he wouldn't have to spoon-feed him now. He tried not to let his gaze linger on the now-bare upper torso and muscular arms. The stranger might be buff and good-looking, but he could still be a psycho or a criminal for all they knew.

Forcing a smile, he put the tray down on the bedside table, removed his and Lee's plates and sandwiches, then moved the tray to their patient's lap. "Here you go. It's only tomato and herb, I'm afraid, nothing too exotic, but it's all we had."

"That's absolutely fine, thank you. I appreciate it." He gazed at Nathan and, unless Nathan was completely mistaken, there was the slightest hint of warmth in his eyes. Maybe he was an all right bloke, after all. Hopefully it wouldn't be too long before they found out.

They were silent for some time then, as they ate their respective meals, drank their respective drinks. The silence remained for a while after that, too, with the exception of gently clanking cutlery and crockery as Lee gathered up all the used plates and mugs, put them on the tray and returned them to the kitchen.

Nathan was suddenly impatient. Perhaps having a full belly had galvanised him, he didn't know, but what he *did* know was that this stupid limbo couldn't continue. "So," he said, firmly but not aggressively, "we've rescued you, warmed you up, fed and watered you... I think it's about time you told us exactly what happened. And who you are."

Clearing his throat, the man shuffled back a little bit and leaned against the headboard. Nathan resisted the temptation to ask if he wanted more pillows—it would just delay things further, and he wanted answers *now*.

"Yes," the man eventually said, his expression reluctant, "but don't you think we ought to wait for—? Ah, never mind."

Lee entered the room just then, and had clearly caught the tail end of the conversation. He waved a hand. "Please, continue."

"Well..." The stranger glanced from Nathan to Lee, who were each perched on the end of the bed, either side of his feet. "My name's Jonny Sykes."

Nathan inclined his head, encouraging Jonny to continue. *Well, this is progress. Assuming he's telling the truth, that is.*

"I'm, uh... a soldier. In the army. But I think you probably guessed that already."

Failing to hide his irritation, Nathan snapped, "Yes, we'd worked that one out. So, *Jonny,* what the hell happened? How have you ended up in the spare bed in our holiday cottage?"

Jonny frowned and rubbed his eyes. For a moment, an expression of utter despair passed over his features, and Nathan was reminded that, no matter what had taken place, the man was poorly. Granted, no longer in any danger, but still very unwell. He sighed and pinched the bridge of his nose. "I'm sorry, Jonny, I didn't mean to bite your head off. It's just… I'm sure you can see how dodgy this all looks, can't you? Lee and I simply want to know the truth."

"Yeah," he replied resignedly, "I get it. And I'm sorry. For inconveniencing you, ruining your day. I really *am* called Jonny Sykes, by the way. If you get my dog tags, I can prove it to you."

"Your dog tags?" Lee cut in. "You didn't have any on you, mate. That's why we didn't know your name."

"Huh?" Jonny's brow furrowed. "Where the fuck have they gone, then? God, they could be anywhere out there… Not that it matters anymore, I suppose." He cleared his throat again. "*Anyway…* I'm a British soldier, and I was out on exercise. And while I was traipsing over the moorland, through the woods, down ravines and gullies… something happened. I'm not sure I can explain it, really. It sounds clichéd, but I had an epiphany, I suppose. I suddenly wondered what the fuck I was doing there, clumping around in the pissing-down rain and howling wind."

He paused, scratched his head. "I was freezing cold and miserable. Come to think of it, I was probably coming down with the hypothermia, maybe even getting a little delirious. Either way, I decided I'd had enough. I wanted *out*. I gradually let myself drop further and further back from the rest of the group, until I was out of sight. Then I scarpered in the other direction, out of the military training area. I probably wasn't thinking rationally at that point… Everything's a bit of a blur after that. It's possible I threw the dog tags away deliberately." Squeezing his eyes tightly shut, he seemed to be thinking. "I've got vague memories… snippets of climbing, of hiking, more rain, thunder and lightning… A pond, or pool. That's about it, until I woke up here."

Nathan and Lee exchanged a glance. The tiniest tweak of Lee's eyebrow told Nathan that his partner agreed with him—Jonny was telling the truth. They'd seen how poorly he'd been when they'd found him, so delirium, confusion, was entirely possible.

Lee spoke then. "Well, that makes sense. There was an almighty storm… for most of the day, actually." He glanced out of the window at the slowly darkening sky, the sun creeping westwards towards the horizon. "We'd been stuck indoors for hours. Then, when the weather cleared up, we went for a wander down to a nearby pond, about fifteen minutes' walk away. We found you there and brought you back. No bloody mobile signal, otherwise we'd have phoned an ambulance."

"In this case, that's a good thing," Jonny replied.

"Why?" Nathan asked.

"Because…" He took a deep breath. "I could get into serious trouble for what I've done. Once someone realises I haven't turned up at the rendezvous point, they'll start searching for me. And they're not going to find me, are they? Not out there, anyway. They'll be wasting time and resources, and will be wondering if I'm injured or dead somewhere, or if I've gone AWOL. And the longer I leave it, the worse it will get."

"You, uh… seem to be thinking pretty clearly now," Nathan said. "Can't you get in touch with someone and let them know you're all right? If you give us a number to contact, one of us could go to the farm down the road and ask to use their landline. Way I see it, you were coming down with something, delirious… You weren't yourself. I mean, who in their right mind would bugger off by themselves in a raging thunderstorm? You could have died. You might have, if we hadn't found you."

Jonny pressed his lips together for a moment, then said, "I might have. I really am very grateful, you know. It must have been a bit scary finding me. And how the hell did you get me here, anyway? The place is a fifteen-minute walk away, you say?"

"Yeah," Lee cut in. "It *was* scary. Especially since neither of us had our phones on us. Obviously we didn't know at that point there was no frigging signal. Nathan legged it back here and fetched a duvet and a blanket, and came back to us in the car. We used the duvet as a stretcher and somehow got you in the back seat. I'm surprised we didn't smash your head, actually. So... should one of us head to the farm? Do you have a number?"

"I do, but I'm not sure I want you to use it. Not just yet, anyway."

Lee narrowed his eyes. "Why not?"

"Like I say, I could get into a lot of trouble for what I've done. If they decide I've gone AWOL, anyway. I need some time to think, figure out what I want, what to do next. Can you give me that?"

"How much time are we talking?" Lee's tone was suspicious.

"Just... a couple more days? I know I'm asking a lot, especially since you guys are on holiday. But I'm definitely on the mend now, so you won't have to look after me anymore. I won't be any trouble. You'll hardly know I'm here. Just pretend I'm not, even."

"If we do that," Lee said dryly, "you're gonna be fucking hungry. We'll have to go and get some food in. Unless you want to risk being seen eating in a pub. Is the army likely to put out photographs of you on the news, or anything?"

Shrugging, Jonny said, "I honestly don't know. I've never gone AWOL before. I don't know how long they'd spend looking for me, assuming I'd been hurt or lost. Then how long it would take before they'd give up and decide I'd buggered off. Then widen the search, contact the press, my family, my friends… I just don't know. My brain hurts! It's all whirling around in there, driving me mad. Do you think… you could just give me a couple of days? There's no way you guys will get into trouble. Whatever I decide, we can just say I was delirious for a few days, and that you didn't know who I was or where I came from. No comeback on you at all."

"It's a big ask, mate," Lee said. "We need to talk about this, all right?"

"Of course. I completely understand. I'd be the same in your position."

Lee stood, and Nathan followed his lead. This time, confident Jonny was well enough that nothing untoward would happen if they didn't watch him, they closed the bedroom door before heading to the living room and sitting side by side on the sofa.

"Well?" Lee asked.

Nathan huffed out a heavy breath and ran a hand through his hair. "Well, I do believe him. So that's something. I just… I dunno, it's all a bit out of my comfort zone. And what if he's wrong? What if we *can* get into trouble? Even if he was delirious, if we didn't know who he was or where he'd come from, wouldn't we at least phone the police? A doctor?"

"No signal, remember?"

"The farm?"

Lee thought for a moment. "Too scared to leave him, in case something happened."

"Why didn't we take him straight to a hospital?"

"We… suspected hypothermia and wanted to get him into the warm as soon as possible? We got him here, thought we'd phone an ambulance once we arrived, but had no signal?"

Nathan rolled his eyes. "We're going to have to get our story straight, Lee, all three of us. And make sure we sound plausible, and that we stick to it. Otherwise, we're fucked."

"Agreed. I just feel kinda sorry for the bloke. Sounds like he really doesn't know what he wants, and giving him a day or two thinking time could really help him out. Help him make the right decision for his future. We've both had jobs we hated in the past, haven't we? And I'm assuming it's more complicated than giving a month's notice in his case."

"Yeah, probably. So, are you going to tell him, or am I?"

Chapter Five

The next morning, after they'd all eaten breakfast, Nathan and Lee were in the kitchen making a shopping list. "Right," Nathan said, tucking the pen behind his ear, "I'm going to go and see if there's anything else Jonny wants. Back in a mo."

He headed for the spare bedroom, notepad in hand, feeling much happier than he had yesterday. Sure, the situation was still pretty bonkers, but the three of them had had a really long, thorough talk and gone over every what-if they could think of, and come up with an answer. Then, in a stroke of genius, Jonny had even said that, once he'd made his decision, he'd just walk to the farm himself and make the phone call. Nobody else would even need to know Nathan and Lee had helped him.

After knocking on the door, Nathan retrieved the pen from behind his ear, ready for any requests Jonny might have. There was no answer. He waited for a few moments, then knocked again. He might be asleep, or in the en suite bathroom. If it was the former, he'd feel bad for waking him, though he was sure Jonny wouldn't mind, given this was his only opportunity to speak up if there *was* anything particular he wanted from the supermarket.

Nothing. Nathan shifted from foot to foot, his heart rate picking up. What if he *wasn't* asleep or in the bathroom? What if he'd had a relapse? Passed out? Died?

Louder this time, he rapped on the door. "Jonny? Are you in there? Are you all right?" Knocked again. "*Jonny!*"

His panic and wild imagination unwilling to let him wait any longer, he flung open the door and stepped into the room. He felt a slight sense of relief when Jonny wasn't in the bed—not relapsed then—then realised he could have passed out in the bathroom, banged his head on the sink...

He'd taken a single step towards the en suite when he heard a noise—or rather the ceasing of a noise he hadn't noticed before—then the rattle of the door handle. He stood, frozen, as a totally naked Jonny stepped out of the en suite, rubbing a towel over his dripping hair.

Opening his mouth to stutter an apology, he got interrupted when Lee barrelled into the room behind him, almost crashing into his back. "Hey, I heard banging. Is everything all—Oh!"

Jonny glanced at them, seemingly untroubled by the fact he was standing there, completely starkers, and two blokes had just burst into the room and were now gawping at him. A slow, wide smile crept over his face. "All right, lads?"

His face so hot he worried the skin would melt right off, Nathan weakly wafted his notebook in the air. "I'm s-sorry, I just c-came to see if you needed anything from the supermarket. I knocked on the d-door and you didn't reply. I kept knocking, then panicked because I thought you'd got ill again, or passed out and banged your head, or—"

"Hey." Jonny put his hands on his hips, then spoke, his tone gentle, "It's all right, honestly. I get it. And it *is* your place, after all. I'm just an unexpected guest—you can do what you like."

Struggling to keep his eyes on Jonny's face, rather than any of the bits below it, Nathan replied, "Y-yeah, but I didn't mean to invade your, uh, privacy..." He indicated Jonny's nude body with the notebook, then snatched it back towards his chest, cringing.

Jonny shrugged. "It's no bother, honestly. We've all got the same equipment, haven't we? Nothing you haven't seen before, I'm sure." His smile widened, turned lascivious. "Though, thinking about it, maybe I should make you two show me yours, then we'll be even."

Nathan stepped back with a gasp, accidentally bumping into Lee and treading on his foot.

Lee grunted, grabbed Nathan's shoulders from behind and moved him to the side. Then he took two strides towards Jonny and pointed at his face. "Now look here, soldier boy," Nathan couldn't see Lee's face, but the irritation was clear from his body language, even from the back, "you may be all big and muscular, and know how to shoot a fucking gun, but that doesn't give you the right to go around saying things like that. *And* just because you're used to communal showers or whatever doesn't mean it's okay to stand there with your cock and balls flapping about. For God's sake, put your fucking towel around your waist like a normal person!"

"All right, all right." Jonny made short work of covering up, then held his hands aloft. "I'm sorry, okay? I was just having a bit of fun. And… Well, I thought that since you two are an item, you might, uh, occasionally welcome a third person into your bed."

Nathan had watched and listened to the goings on with a dry mouth and—he hoped neither of the other men would notice—a rapidly stiffening cock. Jonny *was* hot, though he wouldn't in a million years have had him down as gay, or bi. But, then, he hardly knew him.

The heady mixture of the charged atmosphere, the mostly naked bloke, and finally, the offer—was it an offer?—of a threesome had made Nathan's dick stiff enough to chop wood. The last thing he wanted to do right now was go to the fucking supermarket.

But how would Lee react? His indignation and anger were obvious and justified, but he hadn't yet said no, or punched Jonny in the face—though that could be more down to self-preservation than a lack of urge to do so. They had, in fact, engaged in idle pillow talk on this very subject on more than one occasion—agreeing that, as long as it was someone they were both attracted to, and that it wouldn't affect their relationship, then having a *ménage à trois* was entirely possible. And desirable. Something they both wanted to tick off their bucket lists.

Silence saturated the room for several more seconds, then Lee seemed to get a grip of himself. "You want a threesome? With us? Well," he moved back towards Nathan and looped an arm around his neck, grinning widely, "I can't say I blame you. But it's a pretty crass way of making a proposition, mate."

"Yeah," Jonny had the good grace to look chagrined, "I know. But it just kinda popped out, you know? I saw an opportunity, and I took it." He paused, peered at Nathan and Lee's faces, then continued, "So, uh, is that a yes or a no, then?" His expression was hopeful and, if Nathan wasn't mistaken, he wasn't the only one sporting an erection. There was an interesting bulge developing beneath Jonny's towel.

Nathan spoke before Lee had the chance. "It's a 'please give us a moment, we need to discuss this,' all right?"

Jonny nodded wordlessly.

Nathan led Lee from the room, closed the door, then headed into their own bedroom. Once that door was secured behind them, Nathan dumped the notebook and pen and turned to look at Lee, willing his erection to subside. He needed the head on his *shoulders* to make this decision, not the one much lower down. "You didn't punch him in the face, so I'm going to go out on a limb and assume you're not dead set against the idea."

Slumping onto the end of their bed, Lee looked up at Nathan. "Honestly, I don't know *what* to think. It's not something that had even entered my head until he said it. I'm having trouble keeping up, yet, at the same time… You're right, I'm not dead set against the idea. And since you're not punching *me* in the face, does that mean you're not, either?"

Nathan thought for a moment, then shrugged. "It's not a terrible idea. It's something we've discussed several times, something we both said we'd like to try. And he ticks our boxes—we both find him attractive and, given we'll never see him again once he's left here, he's not going to affect our relationship."

A small frown line appeared between Lee's eyebrows. "But we don't know when he's leaving."

"Not exactly, no. He said a couple of days. He's clearly feeling better… If he's up to fucking two blokes, then he's up to a walk to the farmhouse down the road. Today, tomorrow, the day after… What does it matter? We all fuck, he leaves whenever, end of story. There's the added bonus of us being on holiday—he's not in our actual home, so we can have fun together, then walk away at the end of the week with nothing but sexy memories. I have no problem with it if you don't. Equally, if you're not up for it, I'm fine with that, too. We have to be absolutely on the same page here."

"Yeah, we do. I think…" He scratched his head. "I think you're right, Nath. This is the perfect opportunity. He's hot, there will be no strings, no one is going to get hurt. We have fun together, then go our separate ways. Well, not you and me, babe, obviously."

"*Obviously.*" Nathan stepped between Lee's legs. "You're not getting rid of me that easily." He leaned down and pressed his mouth hard to Lee's, tangling his fingers in his lover's hair and tugging sharply, knowing the sparks of pain would ramp up Lee's arousal.

Delving his tongue between Lee's lips, Nathan poured all his love and affection into the kiss, hoping Lee would sense it, would know that this potential *thing* with Jonny was about sex, and nothing more. Because with *them*, it was about everything—sex, emotion, adoration, sharing their lives… They were soul mates. And nothing could come between them. Certainly not a hot mess of a soldier they'd found by a bloody pond in the middle of the British countryside.

Pulling reluctantly away after a few minutes, Nathan shook his head a little to regain his focus, then said gently, "So, what do you think? Like I said, we have to be on the same page here. No fuck is worth affecting our relationship for—except maybe Tom Hardy—so we both have to be sure. We should put the poor bloke out of his misery. He probably feels like he's the last one to be picked for the football team."

Lee chuckled. "Once again, you're right. Tom Hardy is *totally* worth affecting our relationship for." He ducked Nathan's swiping hand, then continued, "But this guy isn't. And I don't think he will. Like you say, we have one, two, maybe three days of fun, then we move on. I think," he grinned widely, "you should probably add condoms and lube to the shopping list. Seems we're going to need extra supplies."

Chapter Six

His nerves and uncertainty gone, Nathan grabbed Lee's hands and pulled him to standing. "Come on. Let's go pick Jonny for this football team."

"*Fuck*ball team, you mean?"

Nathan rolled his eyes and punched Lee playfully on the arm. "If you say so."

They returned to the guest room. Despite knowing how stupid and pointless it was, Nathan knocked on the door, shrugging as Lee gave him a questioning glance.

"Come in!"

They entered, and Nathan was surprised—and, if he was honest with himself, a little disappointed—to find Jonny now fully dressed in the clothes they'd lent him. He wore Lee's tracksuit bottoms and one of Nathan's baggiest T-shirts. Being bigger and bulkier than both of them, however, he still looked a little comical—not that Nathan was going to say that out loud. The trousers clung marvellously to his bottom, but were slightly too short in the leg. The T-shirt seemed as though it was barely holding it together, stretched across biceps and pecs as it was. Nathan gulped as the thought flashed through his head that he kind of envied the stressed garment.

"Everything all right?" Jonny asked, his bravado seemingly gone. His eyes were full of uncertainty, and he took an age folding the towel he'd used, before shaking it out and taking it back into the bathroom, presumably to hang it up. When he reappeared, he said, "Well? You guys are killing me here."

Lee looked at Nathan, who nodded.

"Yes," Lee said. "Everything's fine. We were just discussing the situation we find ourselves in. And, well… we're in. It's just a bit of fun, right?"

His eyebrows almost disappearing into his cropped hair, Jonny replied, "Wow, okay. I mean, um, yes, it's just a bit of fun. I have no wish to come between you guys, if you'll pardon the pun. But you're so solid that's not gonna happen. So… uh, great! How do we do this thing? Who tops, who bottoms? Is oral on the table? Kissing?"

"Fucking hell, Jonny," Lee said, "shut up. You're overthinking things. Let's just go with the flow, all right?"

"Yes, yes, of course. Nathan—you're all right with this?"

"Absolutely." He nodded. "But just hold that thought, okay? I'll be back in a sec." He dashed into the main bedroom and retrieved the condoms and lube they *did* have. He'd buy plenty when he eventually got to the supermarket. Though who knew when that would be. He grinned. As excuses for delaying a shopping trip went, it was a pretty fucking good one.

"Okay," he said, hurrying back into the other room, "I'm back, and I brought condoms and lube!" As he held them in the air, he realised he'd probably sounded a bit of a twat, but it was too late to take it back now. And besides, when no doubt totally hot man-on-man-on-man sex was in their immediate future, who the fuck cared about a verbal faux pas?

"Great," Lee replied, flashing him a warm smile. "I'll shut the door."

He moved over to do so, and it was then Nathan realised Lee was nervous, too. Because why the fuck did the door need to be shut? The outside doors to the cottage were closed and locked, nobody could get in, and there was no one around for miles anyway. He bit his lip to prevent a smirk. Lee being nervous was kinda cute, and it made him feel better about his own pounding heart and sweaty palms.

He crossed over to the bed before his nerve failed him, then put the lube and protection on top of the duvet before bending to remove his shoes. When he straightened, Jonny was struggling out of the too-tight T-shirt. He got stuck with the thing half on, half off, and Nathan took the opportunity to admire the exposed abs close up for a moment before moving to help, giggles threatening to bubble from his lips the entire time.

Just as he went to grab the hem of the shirt, Jonny frustratedly yanked it up and ended up smacking Nathan in the face. "Oh, shit!" Jonny said, flinging the top across the room and grabbing Nathan's wrist, pulling away the hand he'd clapped to his mouth. "Are you all right?"

Nathan couldn't help it—as soon as his smile was revealed to Jonny's concerned gaze, the laughter followed. "Fuck, I'm sorry. It's just... The T-shirt was stuck, then you hit me... Like a bloody *Carry On* film or something." He dissolved into guffaws.

Jonny frowned for a second, then seemed to catch the bug. The corners of his mouth tweaked up, his smile growing bigger and bigger, and soon, he too was laughing uncontrollably.

Lee joined them, shaking his head. "You know, they say

laughter and sex go well together… Wanna test the theory?" He began removing his clothes, with Nathan and Jonny watching. The more items he removed, the quicker their mirth faded away. Then, as if a switch had been flipped, there was a race to see who could get naked the fastest.

Lee was first, having taken off most of his clothes as the other two men laughed and watched him. Then Jonny, given he only had the tracksuit bottoms on. They cheered when the last item of Nathan's clothing finally landed on the large pile.

Jonny turned towards the bed, giving the other two men a spectacular view of his arse—high, firm and eminently fuckable. Nathan wondered who would get to go first, if Jonny was into bottoming. He certainly hoped so—he and Lee were happy to fuck any which way, so it'd be nice to have that variety with a third in their bed, too.

After settling into the centre of the bed, Jonny patted the mattress either side of him. "Care to join me?"

With a final glance at each other for confirmation, Nathan and Lee did just that, getting into position either side of the soldier. Before indecision could spoil the charged atmosphere, Nathan said, "Given you smacked me in the mouth, soldier boy, I think you should kiss it better."

Jonny's tentative expression melted away, to be replaced with a predatory look. "With pleasure." He tilted his body towards Nathan, then slipped his hand behind Nathan's neck and pulled him close, so the tips of their noses almost touched. "I'm sorry for hitting you, it was an accident." His hot breath washed over Nathan's lips, cheeks and chin.

Nathan gulped. "You're forgiven. But I still want you to kiss it better."

"Not a problem." The miniscule gap between them disappeared as Jonny captured his lips, melding their mouths together in a kiss that was hot, but surprisingly sweet at the same time. Maybe because they were both kissing someone new, it was tentative, searching, since neither of them knew what the other liked. They teased and titillated, their tongues twining, exploring, thrusting.

Nathan felt a hand on his cock. He jumped a little, thinking how odd it was that Jonny had gone from gentle, sensual lip-locking to cock-grabbing in a millisecond. But then he realised the sensation of the hand on his dick was familiar. There was no guesswork, no testing the waters. This hand knew exactly what it was doing, how to please him.

Groaning into Jonny's mouth, Nathan began jerking into Lee's tight, hot fist. His brain suddenly seemed to catch on to exactly what was happening—*I'm having a fucking threesome!*—and, as a result, his arousal went off the charts. He had to concentrate hard not to lose his shit there and then, and spunk into Lee's hand when they'd barely begun. That would be embarrassing—like a teenage boy, for Christ's sake!

Fortunately, he didn't come, and carried right on enjoying himself, relaxing and beginning to explore Jonny's body with his hands as he was kissed and tossed off… by two different men. *Holy fuck, this is intoxicating.*

Jonny's muscles felt as sexy as they looked, and he smiled

against Jonny's mouth as he reached around to grab his arse and discovered Lee's stiff cock instead, prodding against Jonny's buttocks. There were too many arms, too many hands wandering around to do anything about Lee's cock right now, not without getting into a tangle, so Nathan pulled back and decided to stick with exploring Jonny's cock for the time being. He was confident that, by the time they were done, all three of them would have got plenty of attention.

Jonny's dick was much like the rest of him—long, bulky and hard. Nathan gripped it eagerly, then let it glide in and out of his loose fist to begin with, before squeezing it more tightly. He was gratified when Jonny groaned into his mouth, and his cock thickened in Nathan's hand.

The three of them continued this way for some time, until Nathan broke away from Jonny's kiss with a gasp for air, followed by a growl. "Shit, Jonny, I need to be inside you. Turn over on your side, kiss Lee, and I'll fuck you from behind while you toss each other off."

He didn't know where his sudden bossy streak had come from, but he kinda liked it. Especially when the other two men obeyed eagerly, and were already kissing heatedly by the time he'd retrieved the condoms and lube. He quickly sheathed himself, then slicked plenty of the liquid on his shaft before coating the tips of his fingers, discarding the bottle and searching for Jonny's rear entrance.

After finding what he sought, he dabbed lube on Jonny's hole, before slowly breaching the entrance and working some of it inside him. At the same time, he watched Jonny kissing and tossing off Lee, while Lee did the same to Jonny. The sight ramped up his arousal further, and he let out a growl before gripping the base of his own shaft and butting the head up against Jonny's arsehole. He paused for a moment to give Jonny a chance to protest, then pushed on when there was none. Slowly, carefully, he passed through the tight grip of Jonny's sphincter, the lube easing his way, breathing hard and digging his fingers into Jonny's hip.

The combined grunts, groans and heavy breaths from the three of them filled the air, mingling and seeming to feed off one another. The sounds climbed to a crescendo as the action heated up—Lee and Jonny still snogging each other's faces off as they wanked each other, while Nathan pounded Jonny's dark, delicious hole, the whole time drinking in the view of his partner being masturbated by a virtual stranger.

Soon, his balls boiled and he could hold on to his climax no longer. The sensations—both physical and mental—and the erotic act that played out in front of him were just too much. It was like watching and acting in a porn film at the same time. Gripping harder onto Jonny's hip, he fucked his arse faster and harder, then pushed his face into the crook between Jonny's neck and shoulder as he hovered on the very precipice of coming. He was held there, suspended, for several seconds, then he plummeted over with a yell. After a beat, he sank his teeth into Jonny's shoulder.

Apparently enjoying the pain, Jonny tore his face away from Lee's and let out a roar. Even as he rode out his own orgasm, Nathan watched Jonny's cock twitch in Nathan's fist before it released its load over the duvet and Lee's fist and stomach.

"Baby," Nathan uttered, hardly knowing what he was about to say. But apparently his brain did. He and Lee made eye contact, and Nathan's cock throbbed at the longing he saw in his lover's eyes. "Come for me. Please."

With a bob of his head, Lee closed his eyes and sank his teeth into his bottom lip. His entire body seemed to freeze, then, after a few seconds, he let out a string of expletives as he came. Jet after jet of spunk flew out, Lee grunting with each one.

Eventually, the three of them came down from their respective climaxes and began to disentangle. Nathan carefully eased out of Jonny's arse, holding the base of the condom secure. Then he headed for the en suite to get rid of it and wash up.

When he returned, Jonny and Lee hadn't moved much, just rolled onto their backs and stared at the ceiling as they attempted to get their breath, return their heart rates to normal. There was a touch of awkwardness in the air. Nathan decided to try to dispel it. "Hey, guys." He waited until they both turned to him. "How many condoms and how much lube should I put on the shopping list, then?"

Fortunately, his not-really-a-joke did its job, and the three of them burst into laughter. Nathan clambered back onto the bed, then insinuated himself between the two men. "What? I'm serious! There's only one condom left, and it's my turn to get fucked, so you two had better make up your minds…"

Four hands reached for Nathan's eager body. As he let the two other men have their way with him, Nathan smiled to himself, figuring that he and Lee were going to have plenty of fodder for their occasional dirty-talk sessions for months, possibly years to come.

Their sexy soldier boy would be gone, but not forgotten. He'd certainly been a most interesting find.

*****

A note from the author: Thank you so much for reading *Magnificent Manlove*. If you enjoyed it, please do tell your friends, family, colleagues, book clubs, and so on. Also, posting a short review on the retailer site you bought the book from (as well as Goodreads and BookBub, if you have them) would be incredibly helpful and very much appreciated. There are lots of books out there, which makes word of mouth an author's best friend, and also allows us to keep doing what we love doing—writing.

About the Author

Lucy Felthouse is the award-winning author of erotic romance novels *Stately Pleasures* (named in the top 5 of Cliterati.co.uk's 100 Modern Erotic Classics That You've Never Heard Of), *Eyes Wide Open* (winner of the Love Romances Café's Best Ménage Book 2015 award), *The Persecution of the Wolves, Hiding in Plain Sight,* and *The Heiress's Harem* and *The Dreadnoughts* series. Including novels, short stories and novellas, she has over 170 publications to her name. Find out more about her writing at **http://lucyfelthouse.co.uk**, or on **Twitter (@cw1985)** or **Facebook (http://www.facebook.com/lucyfelthousewriter)**. Join her **Facebook group (https://www.facebook.com/groups/lucyfelthousereadergroup)** for exclusive cover reveals, sneak peeks and more! Sign up for automatic updates on **Amazon (http://author.to/lucyfelthouse)** or **BookBub (https://www.bookbub.com/authors/lucy-felthouse)**. Subscribe to her newsletter here: **http://www.subscribepage.com/lfnewsletter**

If You Enjoyed Magnificent Manlove

I hope you enjoyed reading *Magnificent Manlove* as much as I enjoyed writing it. If so, you may also like these other M/M books. My full backlist is on **my website (http://lucyfelthouse.co.uk)**.

Desert Heat & Native Tongue

Desert Heat:

Their love is forbidden by rules, religion and risk. Yet still they can't resist.

Captain Hugh Wilkes is on his last tour of duty in Afghanistan. The British Army is withdrawing, and Wilkes expects his posting to be event-free. That is, until he meets his Afghan interpreter, Rustam Balkhi, who awakens desires in Wilkes that he'd almost forgotten about, and that won't be ignored.

Native Tongue:

They may be back on British soil, but the battle isn't over.

When Captain Hugh Wilkes fell for his Afghan interpreter, Rustam Balkhi, he always knew things would never be easy. After months of complete secrecy, their return to England should have spelt an end to the sneaking around and the insane risks. But it seems there are many obstacles for them to overcome before they can truly be happy together. Can they get past those obstacles, or is this one battle too many for their fledgling relationship?

More information and buy links: https://lucyfelthouse.co.uk/published-works/desert-heat-native-tongue/

Doctor's Orders

Hospital porter Aaron Miller isn't expecting a very exciting birthday. He and his doctor boyfriend, Blake Colville, are working opposite shifts, leaving Aaron to go home to an empty house and the prospect of another shift the following day. Just as he's leaving work, however, an unexpected sexy encounter in a supply cupboard leaves him feeling in a much more celebratory mood. And an impending dirty weekend away with Blake just puts the icing on the non-existent cake. But who needs cake when you're dating a dominant doctor?

More information and buy links: https://lucyfelthouse.co.uk/published-works/doctors-orders/

Love on Location

When Theo Samuels heads off to film on location in the village of Stoneydale, he's expecting drama to take place on camera, not off. But when he meets gorgeous local lad, Eddie Henderson, he struggles to ignore his attraction. A relationship between the two of them would be utterly impractical, yet they're drawn together nonetheless. Can they overcome the seemingly endless hurdles between them? Or is their fling destined to remain as just that?

More information and buy links: https://lucyfelthouse.co.uk/published-works/love-on-location/